"Morgan, you've got to stop this."

"Jason! How nice to hear from you. How are you?"

"Terrible. Do you have any idea how embarrassing it is to be on the receiving end of all these 'gifts' you keep sending me?"

She gave him an impish grin through the telephone. "I thought you'd enjoy them."

"These ferns—"

"I've always felt that a person can't have too many ferns, don't you agree?"

"Morgan, enough is enough." In spite of his stern voice, Jason sounded as if he were very close to breaking into a laugh. "But, I'll give you an 'A' for originality and cleverness."

"How about for persistence?"

"*Especially* for persistence—but it's all got to stop. You're disrupting my office. My employees can hardly get any work done, what with their damned twittering about the things that are constantly arriving and their speculation about what you're going to do next." There was a significant pause. "What *are* you going to do next?"

WHAT ARE *LOVESWEPT* ROMANCES?

They are stories of true romance and touching emotion. We believe those two very important ingredients are constants in our highly sensual and very believable stories in the *LOVESWEPT* line. Our goal is to give you, the reader, stories of consistently high quality that may sometimes make you laugh, sometimes make you cry, but are always fresh and creative and contain many delightful surprises within their pages.

Most romance fans read an enormous number of books. Those they truly love, they keep. Others may be traded with friends and soon forgotten. We hope that each *LOVESWEPT* romance will be a treasure—a "keeper." We will always try to publish

LOVE STORIES YOU'LL NEVER FORGET
BY AUTHORS YOU'LL ALWAYS REMEMBER

The Editors

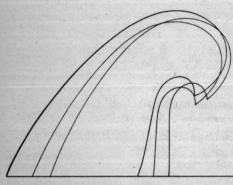

LOVESWEPT • 21

Fayrene Preston

The Seduction of Jason

BANTAM BOOKS • TORONTO • NEW YORK • LONDON • SYDNEY

THE SEDUCTION OF JASON

A Bantam Book / October 1983

LOVESWEPT and the wave device are trademarks of
Bantam Books, Inc.

ISBN 0-553-21622-8

Published simultaneously in the United States and Canada

Bantam Books are published by Bantam Books, Inc. Its
trademark, consisting of the words "Bantam Books" and the
portrayal of a rooster, is Registered in U.S. Patent and
Trademark Office and in other countries. Marca Registrada.
Bantam Books, Inc., 666 Fifth Avenue, New York, New
York 10103.

PRINTED IN THE UNITED STATES OF AMERICA

O0 9 8 7 6 5 4 3 2 1

One

Morgan Saunders sank into the narrow seat and shut her eyes with a groan. The double Scotch she had just consumed in the airport lounge should have calmed her down. Sami had said it would. But then Samuelina Adkinson, her slightly bizarre next-door neighbor and long-time friend, said a lot of things.

It had been Sami who had said, "You've been working too hard and need a vacation. You've always wanted to go to the Caribbean, so why not go now?" She had also said, "Who knows? You may meet a tall, dark stranger who'll sweep you off your feet."

Morgan ran her hand shakily through her shoulder length ash-blond hair. *When* was she going to stop listening to Sami?

Leaning her head back against the headrest, she

squeezed her eyes shut and her forehead pleated in frustration. She really hated this fear she had of flying. She didn't like to think of herself as a neurotic person, even though she had to admit that sometimes her actions were governed by vague anxieties, weird compulsions, or even magnificent obsessions. This trip was a prime example of that. Even so, she had always tried to maintain a balance between the seeming contradictions in her nature, and, emotionally, she tended to think of herself as a very stable person.

The supersized jet idled throbbingly with the energy of its internal environmental system. But though the marvel of the plane's technology should have reassured her, it only frightened Morgan to think of just how many things there were on such a big, complex system that could go wrong.

This was a late night flight and the passengers were exuding a holiday gaiety as they settled into their seats around her. Wishing with all her heart that she could relax and join in their enthusiasm, Morgan realized that, tonight, it was no use. She was scared to death of flying and a double Scotch or ten double Scotches was not going to cure her of it.

Normally she avoided flying like the plague, either taking the train or the bus or sometimes even a ship. But this time, because of her business, it hadn't been sensible. And Morgan was usually very sensible—"usually" being the catch word.

She had waited until the last minute to board the aircraft, and had quickly taken the window seat she'd asked to have assigned to her. She didn't want to have to get up to let anyone enter her row. But she had no desire to look out that window either, knowing what she would see. Deep in the heart of winter, snow had iced over St. Paul with a frosting of white. According to the weather report, more snow was expected tomorrow and it was this very harshness and the bone-chilling cold accompanying it that she wished to escape for a couple of weeks.

Morgan had reserved a seat in the back row which the man at the desk had told her was empty. She was hoping for privacy. If she was going to make a fool of herself, she wanted to be alone. But just as that thought occurred, a slight sound of movement, a gentle poof of warm air and aroma that whiffed toward her, all indicated that someone had taken the seat beside her.

Fear was supposed to heighten the senses, yet she hadn't been able to tell that the aisle seat on her row had been filled. Obviously it had, however, because someone had evidently been forced to sit in the middle seat beside her.

Morgan attempted to ignore her new seatmate, trying to think some positive thoughts about the safety of flying. The airline industry was always throwing out statistics about their safety versus that of other forms of travel. Unfortunately, she couldn't seem to recall any at the moment—maybe because, for some odd reason, the person sitting next to her kept intruding into her consciousness.

The scent permeating the air around her was unmistakably masculine—clean, cool, fresh and slightly woodsy. But man or no man, tantalizing odor or no tantalizing aroma, Morgan did not intend to open her eyes. And she certainly did not intend to engage in idle chitchat when she was about to die! She could see the headlines now. "Owner of 'Little Bit Of Paradise' Killed in Plane Crash."

Feeling the brush of fine wool against her forearm, Morgan's thoughts were once more drawn back to her seatmate. He must be wearing tweed, she arbitrarily decided, expensively soft. Wonder what the odds were that he was tall, dark and handsome? Astronomical, no doubt.

On the other hand, the tall part might be right; he could be a big man, because he seemed to be having some trouble getting comfortable in the narrow coach seat. Surmising that the man was taller than her own five foot seven because she felt his shoulder bump against her when he shifted in his seat, Morgan tried to picture what else he looked like.

The first jolt of movement from the plane startled her out of this speculation. Tightening her hold on the armrests, she tried to imagine her warm, sun-drenched destination, rather than the fact that the plane was moving out onto the runway. Sami had said that the beauty of Martinique would be well worth the terror of the airplane ride . . . but then what did Sami know?

That particular thought led, maddeningly, back to Sami's prophecy and thus to the man next to her. Without opening her eyes, she seemed to be absorbing this unknown person through her senses. This was ridiculous! Nothing like it had ever happened to her before.

The momentary pressure of a hard, muscled thigh against hers made Morgan guess that he was obviously a man in good physical condition. But straining to hear his motions, she heard only the creaks and groans of the plane as it moved, and having read somewhere that the greatest danger of a crash came at takeoff and landing, Morgan cursed silently. She had to get her mind off the man next to her and back onto the effort of getting this paralyzing fear of hers under control.

Why, oh why, had she listened to Sami? Morgan didn't want to die. She was only twenty-six and her business had just begun to pay off this past year.

The bright, flirtatious voice of a stewardess pierced her panic-stricken mind. "Mr. Falco. What are you doing sitting here? You're supposed to be in First Class. Couldn't you find your seat?"

A deep, firm voice answered, "I decided I would rather sit back here."

"But I'm sure you'd be more comfortable in First Class. Let me show you to your seat."

"Thank you all the same, but I'll stay right here."

Well, Morgan reflected, at least he was polite—in a commanding sort of way—but definitely someone used to doing exactly as he pleased. The voice had been young, too. Oh, not too young, but not too old either. The age thirty-five stuck in her mind for no reason at all.

The big jet, like some prehistoric dinosaur out of its natural element, had begun to lumber down the runway, getting into position for takeoff.

The same stewardess who had spoken to the unseen Mr. Falco now came on the intercom. "Welcome to the charter, nonstop flight of World Airways to Fort-de-France, Martinique. We're happy to have you with us this evening and hope your flight will be a pleasant one. At this time, I would like to introduce our crew. Our captain's name is Robert "Slick" Williams, our co-pilot's name is . . ."

Slick! Morgan's mind reeled at the name. How could she trust a pilot who had a name like "Slick"?

As the stewardess continued her little spiel, Morgan chose not to listen. Knowing that the pilot had a cutsey nickname did not inspire a lot of confidence and she felt as though she would need to use all her powers of concentration to help him get the plane off the ground and to keep it up in the air.

The plane came to a halt, then sat at the end of the runway while the jets roared in preparation for its final lunge down the long strip of concrete.

Morgan took the moment of reprieve to rub her sweaty palms over the skirt of her tailored dress, speculating silently on her chances of getting the powers-that-be to turn the plane around, take it back to the terminal and let her out. She wouldn't even ask for a refund.

Too late! The big jet began to roll, gathering speed, and Morgan's hands grabbed for something solid. Her left hand took a death grip on an armrest, but her right came down on top of a large hand. Flinching only momentarily at the unexpected contact, she fastened onto the warm security of it. "Any port in a storm" became her new motto suddenly, as she noticed the pleasing tactile sensation of the hairs on the back of the large, muscular hand.

The plane was hurling headlong down the runway at a terrifying speed and Morgan felt as if her body were being plastered against the seat. Hearing her heart hammering loudly, she realized her breathing rate had increased drastically. Sami, she thought to herself, I'll never understand how I let you talk me into this.

All at once, she felt another large hand come down on top of hers and her seatmate's calm voice saying, "We'll be all right, you know. There's nothing to be afraid of."

His palm felt smoothly uncalloused against the back of her hand and, as the big jet catapulted into the sky, a small measure of the man's confidence began to seep through to her from the reassuring pressure of his hand.

The plane began its steep ascent and Morgan found herself in the irrational position of being torn between her fear of being airborne and her fascination with a man she had never seen. Extraordinary as it seemed, no matter how much she had tried to shut this person out, he had somehow succeeded in reaching out to her, assailing her senses and invading her mind—all before they had even looked at one another!

Nevertheless, she kept her eyes closed until the plane finished its climb and leveled off, not daring to open them until she heard the "no smoking" sign *ping* off.

Her vision focused slowly. The first sight she saw were the unfamiliar pair of hands sandwiching her own. They were indeed large, with dark hairs growing across the back and a skin tone of golden copper.

Taking his top hand away, the man turned his

other hand palm up to clasp hers lightly in a new hold.

Now she could see a heavy gold watch around his wrist and part of the brown tweed of his jacket sleeve. Her eyes trailed downward to view a pair of long legs covered with coffee-colored slacks and crossed at the knee. So far so good.

Retracing her route, Morgan turned her head cautiously and encountered a pair of brown eyes looking out at her from an arrestingly attractive face. Parted on the side, his dark brown hair was brushed appealingly back across his well-shaped head and he had an intriguing cleft chiseled into the middle of his well-defined chin. *Definitely*, tall, dark and handsome!

Morgan smiled slowly at the man, for some unexplained reason feeling instantly at ease with him. "I would have been disappointed if you had looked any other way."

His full, sensual mouth turned upward into a grin. "I couldn't lose. I had a bet going with myself that you would either have blue or green eyes, and now I can see that they're blue-green."

Morgan's attention switched curiously to the vacant seat beside him. Not only that, the row across from them was unoccupied!

"I heard the stewardess talking to you. Are you supposed to be in First Class?"

The gold flecks in his eyes seemed to sparkle for her. "My ticket does say First Class, but when I saw you in the lounge, belting down that Scotch, I decided it would be more fun to sit with you."

Laughter lurked in her voice as Morgan inquired politely, "Do you often do things like this?"

"I have to admit I don't. Most of the time, I'm too wrapped up with my work. What about you? Is this an everyday occurrence for you?"

"What?" she bantered easily. "Finding a tall, dark and handsome man beside me?"

"I should imagine that you often find men of all descriptions around you."

Morgan's face colored slightly at his compliment, but she chose to ignore the remark. "I don't usually drink like that. It's just that I'm terribly afraid of flying."

"I noticed," he commented dryly.

Morgan looked down at her hand still clasped in his. "Thanks for the moral support. I suppose a psychiatrist would say I need extensive analysis, and I know that my mother views my fear of flying as a major flaw in my character."

"Your mother?"

"My mother is a very proper Bostonian. Her life is devoted to my father, her clubs and charities and improving me—in that order."

His hand reached out to tilt her chin up, and he studied her face thoughtfully through half-closed eyes. "It doesn't look as if there's too much wrong with you."

Morgan grinned. "I like to think there's not. But you see, I have a checkered past. I committed a huge indiscretion, almost unforgivable in fact, and my mother never lets me forget it."

"I *knew* I was going to like you. What did you do?"—He actually looked hopeful!—"Murder someone?"

"Oh, no. That she could have forgiven. You see, my parents' very best friends in the whole world, another leading family of Boston, have a son my age. We grew up together and it was expected that we would eventually marry."

"I see." He nodded sagely.

"Exactly. Not that Sebastian wasn't a very nice person."

"Sebastian!"

Morgan giggled at his arched brows. "The only problem was that I didn't love Sebastian. He was too much like a brother."

"I'd like to go on record as saying I understand perfectly."

This man is *absolutely charming*! Morgan thought, and gave him a lovely smile in appreciation of the fact. "Unfortunately my parents didn't. Or at least mother didn't. If it had been just my dad, I might have been able to get around him."

"Daddy's little girl, huh?"

Morgan was thoroughly enjoying herself. Remarkably, she had forgotten all about her deathly fear of flying. Feeling the warmth of her hand in his and seeing the golden glow in his brown eyes, she continued talking to him as if she had known him all her life.

"Dad was generally on my side," she admitted. "Or maybe it would be closer to the truth to say that he was just too busy to really make a fuss, one way or the other. But Mother accused me of having him wrapped around my little finger, anyway."

He spread her hand out. "Such a nice little finger, too. It might be an interesting experience to be wrapped around it." He took it up to his mouth, running it across his bottom lip.

A quick thrill of heat ran through her at the touch of his lips on her finger and Morgan's heart skipped a beat or two. The atmosphere between them had just shifted perceptibly. All at once, their brief relationship seemed to be put on a new plane.

"You didn't marry him, did you?" His deep voice had taken on a softer timbre.

"N-no, I didn't. Sebastian would have been willing to marry me just to please everyone. He was a very passive sort of person and liked me as well as he did anything or anyone else, but I had developed a great crush on my art instructor in college and, in a fit of rebellion, I ran off with him."

Morgan looked confusedly at the man next to her. His grip on her hand hadn't tightened and the expression on his face hadn't changed, but for some reason, she got the impression that he was waiting for what she was about to say next. She hunched her shoulders unconsciously. "The relationship didn't last, naturally. It didn't take long to realize that, well, not only didn't I love him, but the only thing he was in love with was . . . my parent's money."

As hard as it was to talk about, Morgan felt somehow as though it were quite normal to be telling him something that she hadn't spoken about in years—although she had deliberately left out a few very pertinent facts.

"How long ago was that?"

"Six years. I left Boston 'to make it on my own,' as the saying goes."

"And have you?"

She nodded. "I've made a success out of a specialty store that features items from the tropics such as art, shells, plants, rattan, straw, that sort of thing."

His eyes roamed over her face, taking in the peach glow of her skin and the aquamarine beauty of her eyes. Then he spoke very quietly. "What's your name?"

"Name?" She looked at him blankly.

"I don't know your name."

They didn't know each other's names. How absurd! Here she was, flying through the night to the Caribbean, telling a man she had never met before the story of her life. Morgan could only imagine what her mother would say if she knew. But then, her mother wasn't here, was she?

"My name is Morgan Saunders."

He brought the back of her hand to his mouth in a disturbingly personal salute. "How do you do, Morgan Saunders. I'm Jason Falco, and I consider myself a very lucky man to have taken this flight tonight."

Morgan inclined her head. "It's a pleasure, Mr. Falco. Your name sounds familiar. Didn't I read recently that you had been elected to the Board of Directors of the St. Paul Committee on the Fine Arts?"

He moved his head in an affirmative motion. "That's right. So now that you know I have a somewhat reliable reputation and I've heard about the unforgivable indiscretion you committed, let's get comfortable." Reaching down on either side of him, he lifted the arm rests up and out of the way. "There. Now we can have a little more room."

Except he seemed to move closer!

"You're a very interesting lady, Morgan." Holding up his free hand, he ticked off points one by one. "You have a name that could belong to a linebacker—yet you're deliciously feminine. You're a smart, practical businesswoman, having made a success of your own business—yet you're kooky enough to own a South Sea curio shop in the frozen climes of St. Paul, Minnesota. You're fearless enough to go after what you want—yet you're scared to death of plane flights."

He held up her hand again, examining it thoroughly, running his thumb and forefinger slowly and sensuously up and down each of her fingers, spending a great deal of time on each one. "I can't wait to discover more about you."

A wonderfully warm sensation curled in the pit of Morgan's stomach. Jason Falco had the curious power to make her feel as if all things were possible. Outside the airplane, the sky was midnight black; inside, the stewardesses had finished serving and the small population of the plane had begun to settle down for the night. It seemed more than a little ridiculous, but Morgan felt as if she were about to be born anew.

She hadn't related the full story of the art instructor, Clinton Monroe, but it was the reason Morgan had felt such shock at her immediate response to a man she didn't know. Her first night with Clinton had been a traumatic experience for the young, innocent girl she had been then. Clinton had taken her willingness to run away with him as experience, and his lovemaking had been one-sidedly brutal. Afterwards he had accused her of being cold, and nothing had happened in the intervening years to change her mind. She had dated, but she had met no one who could make her care whether she was really frigid or not—until now.

There was David, of course. David DeWitt. They had been dating for a few months. The problem was that David was quite serious about their relationship and she wasn't. He was a very nice person, but when he kissed her goodnight, he left her nearly as cold as Clinton had. To make matters worse, David sensed her indifference and lately had been pushing for marriage as the solution. He just couldn't seem to take her "no" seriously though Morgan had tried to break off with him many times.

"Where are you?" The deeply exciting voice brought her thoughts back to the man sitting next to her.

"Right here." She smiled at him.

His hand ran up the bare skin of her arm. "Tell me, is there someone waiting for you back in St. Paul?"

Just for a moment, the image of David flashed before her—nice, sincere David—and she chewed on her bottom lip indecisively.

The lights had lowered in the cabin, the majority of the people electing to sleep their way through the night hours until they reached their destination. Blankets and pillows were available above every seat and Jason had already stretched up and pulled down a few for them. Morgan, sitting at an angle facing him, with her back resting against the window, reflected on their situation. It was an oddly intimate setting, with Jason and herself isolated in their own little area of three reclining seats and one very dim light overhead—a self-contained island in the sky.

Jason reached out a forefinger to the lip caught between her teeth, releasing it from her grip and soothing the teeth marks away with the pad of his finger. "Don't do that." The command, in itself, was a husky caress.

His touch made up her mind.

"No," she assured him breathlessly. "There's no one."

He leaned toward her with his hand going around the back of her head. The light pressure of his lips stroked back and forth over hers, bringing a surge of unfamiliar emotions tumbling through her.

Morgan went motionless, experiencing the novelty of the sparkling bubbles of hot delight skidding along her veins. There was nothing whatsoever cold about her reaction to Jason and her heart sang with the wonder of it.

Sensing something wrong, he pulled away slightly. "What is it?"

"Nothing," she denied quite honestly. "Nothing at all."

"Here." He stood up and flicked out their light. "Change places with me."

Morgan scooted past and he sat back down, gathering her across his lap. Pulling the blanket up over them, he cuddled her against him. "Now," he questioned softly. "Where were we?"

"You forgot?"

"No. But I decided to leave it up to *you* to tell *me*."

Morgan looked deep into Jason's brown and gold eyes and what she saw comforted her. Although he knew something was wrong, he wasn't going to push her, evidently willing to let her set the pace. What an unusual man Jason Falco was!

"You were kissing me."

"That's right," he agreed softly, his hand resting just under her breast, his thumb sweeping back and forth. "*I* was kissing *you*. Why?"

Morgan searched her mind and found no reason why she shouldn't tell him, even though the only other person she had ever told was Sami. "The art instructor . . . Clinton . . . I couldn't seem to respond . . . as he thought I should. He said I was cold."

Jason muttered a curse under his breath. Then he lowered his lips to hers, slipping his tongue into her mouth to meet and entwine with her own. A rage of need, so unexpected and so strong that it made her forget everything but the man holding her, jolted through Morgan. There, halfway to heaven, suspended on currents of air, in an isolated, dark corner of the plane, beneath an airline-issued blanket, she arched with aroused abandon against the man she had met such a short time ago. An all-encompassing heat consumed her and her body yielded completely to his.

Jason broke off the kiss and groaned hoarsely against her mouth, "The man was a fool! You're about as cold as the Sahara at noon."

Lifting her head a little, Morgan ran her tongue daringly across his lips. "I *was* cold—with *him*," she murmured, then lay her finger where her tongue had been and moved it experimentally across the velvet firmness of his lip.

He took her finger into his mouth and began sucking gently on it. A sunburst of heat exploded inside her. "Jason," she moaned weakly, "what's happening to me?"

"The same thing that's happening to me and I don't think we should fight it," he said huskily. "Do you?"

She shook her head weakly.

Jason raised his hand to unbutton the front of her dress, then, with his large palm, he covered her breast underneath the lace of her bra. Endless minutes passed as they flew countless miles, but Morgan didn't notice. The fiery weakness that flowed through her body was the most beautiful thing she had ever experienced.

She knew that most people on vacations, who were away in strange places, among people they might never see again, usually let their reserve down. Up until now, it had never entered her mind that the same thing could happen to her. Nevertheless, when she had fallen into her seat, her senses had taken over almost from the first moment, leaving her inhibitions behind, and Morgan had no intention of letting it stop.

"Where are you staying on Martinique?" he questioned softly.

"I'm booked in at a restored French plantation up the coast from Fort-de-France."

"Stay with me at the DeWitt House."

"I-I can't."

A tiny twinge of guilt hit Morgan when she thought of why she couldn't stay at the new luxury hotel he had named. David had wanted her to stay there, too, telling her that he would take care of all the arrangements. But she hadn't wanted to because his family owned that particular chain of hotels. Granted, it was only a short branch on the corporation "tree" that was owned and controlled by David's family, but she felt he still would have taken it as encouragement if she had accepted.

"Why?"

"I'd rather not. I want to stay in something more reminiscent of the history of the island rather than a modern hotel that I could see the duplicate of in St. Paul. Why don't you stay at the place where I'm staying?"

"I have some business meetings scheduled in the next few days at the DeWitt. As soon as I'm finished, though, I'll join you."

Morgan contemplated Jason from beneath her lashes. From the way the stewardess had reacted to him and the manner in which he commanded and dressed, it appeared he could probably have all the women he wanted. Yet, here she was making it easy for him.

Why?

Why not? Morgan answered herself defiantly.

She couldn't help but believe, in some instinctive way, that this type of behavior was as unusual for Jason as it was for her. The last few years she had imposed a rigid code of discipline and work on herself, very rarely giving in to the capricious side of her nature. She had had something she wanted to prove, mainly to herself, and she had. Now she was tired and needed a rest and she could afford to relax.

Tonight was the first night of her vacation—a vacation that would be unburdened by the heavy responsibility of the store and the multiplicity of irrelevancies that she seemed to be so expert in getting bogged down with every day. And if it was with a man with whom she had felt an instant rapport, so much the better.

Their lips joined again in a kiss that lengthened and deepened. The stars rushed by and time passed unnoticed, as they flew out of the darkness toward the sun.

Two

The morning sun shone unrestricted and bright in the clear blue sky above Lamentin Airport. Morgan, waiting outside while Jason collected their luggage, breathed deeply of the sweetly scented air. The tranquil warmth of it came as a benediction after the icy north winds she had left behind just hours before. Already the island's complexion of serenity had taken hold of her.

Martinique had a definite "French" ambience. It almost seemed to Morgan that she might have landed in the country of France, instead of in the middle of the Caribbean, on a lush, emerald island known as the "Pearl of the Antilles," and whose Indian name meant Island of the Flowers. Even now, a kaleidoscope of vibrant colors and a mixture of languages, mostly a patois of French, was reaching her eyes and ears.

Morgan had known that the island was an over-seas department of France, governed by Paris, and that it was the largest and northernmost of the Windward Islands. Weeks ago, as she pored over travel brochures, she had hardly been able to wait until she arrived. Now, however, she found that the excitement of seeing a tropical paradise, which stretched fifty miles long and twenty miles wide, had taken a definite second place to the ela-tion of having met Jason Falco.

Who could explain what had happened between them, even before she had opened her eyes and seen him? She couldn't, and she wasn't sure she wanted to try. After all, close inspection of any natural phenomenon might take the mystery and joy out of it. And she didn't want to do that. Not yet, anyway. She had just landed in paradise—and, as far as she was concerned, *anything* could happen in paradise.

The man who was overwhelming her thoughts appeared with their luggage and deposited the pieces beside her. His hands reached for her shoulders, gripping them lightly. "I missed you!"

Morgan smiled slightly, suddenly a little shy of this magnetic man in the full light of day. "We were only apart about ten minutes."

"But that's the most we've been apart since we met." His brown eyes glowed tenderly at her.

Morgan's mood sobered and she gazed pensively at the man standing in front of her, realizing, not for the first time, just how precipitately their rela-tionship had started. So far, nothing irrevocable had passed between them. Perhaps she should take the opportunity to back off while she could, regroup, thus being able to react more sensibly the next time they met—if there was a next time.

Jason seemed to read her thoughts and he spoke gently, piercing through her confused indecision. "We may have spent most of the time since we've met in the clouds, Morgan, but it started on the ground."

She knew what he meant. When she had first become sensorially aware of Jason, the plane had been standing quite still at the terminal. According to her mother, things like this *weren't* supposed to happen. But it had. And it was no dream. She hadn't slept a minute and the only times she had closed her eyes had been during their kisses. Jason had pervaded her senses and, she was very much afraid, her heart.

"Drive into Fort-de-France with me and have breakfast at the DeWitt," he added softly.

She made a wry face. "I'm so grimy and grubby, I won't feel human until I've had a shower and changed into some cooler clothes."

"You look fine, but if you wish, you can shower and change in my suite." He released her shoulder with one hand and ran a finger under the collar of her dress. His touch seemed completely natural. After all, she had just spent the long night in his arms.

Despite her determination to steer clear of the DeWitt House, the temptation to join him was great. As far as she was concerned, the only serpent in her paradise at the moment was her mother's voice that kept resounding in her head: "Morgan Saunders! The times in your life that you've reacted with haste, you've always lived to regret."

Go away, Mother! Morgan shouted soundlessly. I'm not wrong this time. I *know* I'm not.

And having at last voiced the thought in her head, a remarkable thing happened. All at once, she knew she was right. It was at that precise moment that she made her decision—a decision that did not only involve breakfast.

She opened her mouth to agree with his suggestion, but was interrupted by a young man, who, in spite of his slight build, looked to be around eighteen or nineteen years of age. Even though casually dressed, he carried himself with an unmistakable Gallic self-confidence.

"I'm looking for a Miss Saunders who was to be coming in on a charter flight from the States."

"This is Ms. Saunders," Jason told him.

Relief ran through Morgan at the young man's perfectly spoken English, since she, herself, spoke no French. "Hello." She held out her hand, which he took in a firm grip.

"I am Serge Frontenac, Miss Saunders. My father sent me to pick you up."

"How nice," she exclaimed. "They told me that someone would be picking me up, but I didn't realize it would be the owner's son."

"We are a rather small operation at the moment," Serge responded cheerfully in beautifully enunciated English, which carried only a trace of a French accent. "And we like it that way."

Morgan pointed out her bags to Serge, watching him carry them off toward a station wagon with the words, "Frontenac Plantation" scripted across the side. She turned back to Jason. "I think it would be better if I went on with Serge, since he's come all this way."

"It's all right." He smiled understandingly. "I think I have a meeting in about an hour anyway. But I'll see you in a few days."

"Are you sure?" she asked, not fully certain just what she was asking.

Jason nodded. "If I could, I'd skip these conferences altogether, but I'm afraid it's impossible."

"Will you be able to get accommodations? It's the height of the winter season, you know."

"Oh, I'll be able to find something," he assured her teasingly, drawing her into his arms.

His kiss was one of sure possession, and if there had been any small doubts still lingering in Morgan's mind, Jason's kiss would have dispelled them. But she knew that there were none, and she returned his kiss with equal feeling.

Morgan realized that everything about their behavior was highly unusual for so short an acquaintanceship. But then there was nothing ordinary about the way they responded to each other either. Rather, it was uncommonly exceptional how their bodies seemed to be perfectly attuned and how their senses appeared to be a symphony in pure accord.

And unspoken though the fact might be at this point, they both knew it.

"I'll see you in a few days," Jason promised huskily and then he was gone.

• • •

Morgan couldn't have described later with any detail the drive to the Frontenac Plantation. There were only impressions. Her mind was on Jason and she knew it would remain on Jason throughout the next few days.

Serge showed a mature consideration for her feelings by only occasionally pointing out certain sights. They passed through the outskirts of Fort-de-France, the capital of Martinique. A harmonious jumble of multi-hued buildings, the city exhibited a pleasant blend of modern and French colonial architecture.

As they drove up the main road toward St. Pierre, Morgan looked out over a sparkling azure body of water that stretched as far as she could see. To their right, green hills undulated in tiers up the mountains.

Nearing his home, Serge broke his tactful silence and began to speak proudly. "Our island is dominated in the north by a cluster of volcanic mountains, culminating in the forested volcano, Mt. Pelee. A lower backbone of hills leads through the center of the island to a similar group of mountains in the south. You'll have to rent a car, or borrow one from us, and drive around. Most of our roads are pretty good."

"Thanks, I may do that, but for now, I'd just like to rest."

"And wait for the gentleman you were traveling with?" Serge asked knowingly, with a smile that somehow kept the question from appearing rude.

"Yes," she agreed softly, "I'm going to wait for the gentleman I was traveling with."

"We're nearly to our plantation," he observed.

"How is it you speak such perfect English when you are obviously so very French?"

"My grandfather married an English woman. Consequently, my father is half-English and was educated in his mother's country. He insisted that I have an English education as well. Nevertheless as soon as I finished, I came home. This is where my heart is."

"Tell me about your home," she urged.

"It is an eighteenth-century manor plantation house that has been in the family for generations. We have done extensive remodeling. Originally the house had two stories, with the main floor raised well above the ground by brick piers nine feet high."

"How interesting. I don't believe I've ever heard of anything like that."

"You wouldn't unless you were from the South of your country or had visited that area. I understand some of the old Louisiana plantation homes were built along those same lines."

"That might explain why I've never seen any homes like that. I'm from the North. Why did they build them that way?"

"For two reasons: to escape flooding and to catch any passing breezes. The second floor was used as the main floor and the lower level was left open or else it was partly enclosed for storage purposes. Ours has been enclosed now and we use it for guest rooms.

"Our outbuildings are interesting, too. There's the separate building that was used for the kitchen, of course. We haven't decided what to do with that, yet. But the garçonnière that was originally constructed for the bachelors of the family is being restored to use for more guests. Also, there's a trellised summerhouse and a set of pigeonniers."

Serge pulled the car to a stop in front of a gracefully massive structure. Looking at it, Morgan got a sense of how it must have appeared over two hundred years before. Four long French doors were thrown open to the light gusts of air and there were several people relaxing just outside the doors. A high roof, steeply pitched, swept well out over the deep gallery that ran around all sides of the house, protecting its occupants from heat and glare. Slim colonnettes rose up to meet the roof. The whole mansion had a certain sad drama about it and, at the same time, a beautiful contentment.

For no apparent reason, a lump formed in Morgan's throat as she looked at the elegant old home that had been in the Frontenac's family for over two centuries. What a history the house could tell if it could only speak!

Serge got out and came around to open the door for her, gesturing as he did. "We've added a wing, there, to the right, which houses a modern kitchen and a large room with an adjoining terrace that is used for both dining and dancing."

At that moment, a man, elderly and stout, but nonetheless a replica of Serge, descended the wide, sweeping staircase that served to connect the second floor to the ground.

"Miss Saunders," Serge drew her forward, "I would like you to meet my father, Roger Frontenac. Père, this is our new guest from America, Miss Saunders."

"How do you do, Monsieur Frontenac."

"Very well, and please, call me Roger. My family is very small now, with only Serge and myself left. You are staying at my home, therefore you will be one of my family. You will find we are very informal around here. You simply ask for anything you might want."

"Thank you very much, Roger. That's very gracious of you."

"Not at all. Now," he pivoted briskly to his son, "why don't you get Miss Saunders' bags and take them down to her cottage. I'm sure she is tired from her long flight." He turned back to Morgan. "We have assigned you one of our eight cottages as you requested. You will find it is built on the lines of the former slave cabins. Two simple rooms with a tall sloping roof and large windows for coolness. I think you will be quite comfortable. And you will have your own veranda for privacy."

"It sounds charming, and I know I'm going to love staying here."

"I sincerely hope so. We have not as yet succumbed to all the modern ways. No air conditioning or fresh water swimming pool. But I am confident you will find that the trade winds are genuinely refreshing and that the Caribbean provides the best swimming pool you could possibly want. You will take your meals with us, of course, but if you would like something served in your cottage, you have only to ask."

Morgan held out her hand. "Thank you again, Roger, and please, you must call me Morgan."

The old man bent over her hand in a courtly gesture of parting.

• • •

In the days that followed, Morgan fell even more under the spell of the place at which she had chosen to stay. Her bungalow was a lush haven set amid tropical foliage and offered total privacy. She had only to look out any window or walk out onto her veranda to see hibiscus, oleanders, huge poinsettia trees and blue-flowered jacarandas.

She found that the whole plantation offered a simple, pleasant atmosphere, with informality the keynote. The private beach was about half a mile away, and all she had to do was raise her eyes to see the lapis lazuli sea. And, if anyone had asked her what she was doing, she would have had to answer, *"I am waiting for Jason."*

Serge offered to take her on a tour of the plantation. She refused. Roger proposed several likely routes to drive in order to see the best of the island. She declined. The Frontenac's cafe-au-lait Creole cook, Yvonne, plied her with the best of her seafood cuisine, but Morgan only picked at her food.

Morgan waited patiently, in a state of suspension, knowing that her vacation would not start until Jason joined her. She waited, totally relaxed and very sure that he would come.

And on the fourth night, he did.

Morgan stood alone on her veranda. With only an innocently-white lace dress to cover her body, scooped low over her breasts and floating in tiers to her feet, she felt at one with her surroundings.

The tropical night was speaking to her and she listened, experiencing the ebb and flow of the nature around her. Twilight had come and gone and the night had long since awakened, throwing opaque shadows over most of the leafage that burgeoned around the cottage.

But she didn't feel lonely. She had the sounds of the darkness to keep her company. The tallest of the palms were silhouetted against the blue-black of the night sky, and the gentle *swooshing* of the wind through their feathery fronds became a concert of song, harmonizing with the sound of the ageless, primal rhythm of the Caribbean, rolling in waves onto the shore, just beyond the line of the palms.

Something—some slight sound or a vague feeling of movement—made her turn. It was Jason. He stood at the edge of the veranda, just inside the line of light that spilled out from the open French doors. His cream-colored shirt was opened at the neck, with the long sleeves rolled up to reveal his muscular forearms, and his lightweight beige jacket was hooked on two of his fingers and slung over one shoulder.

In that instant, Morgan acknowledged to herself that she was in love with Jason Falco. Why she hadn't realized it before now she didn't know—except, perhaps, that it seemed almost redundant to even *think* the "word" love, when she had been *feeling* the "emotion" love, ever since Jason had first penetrated her screen of fear and seeped into her mind, sitting beside her on the airplane.

Neither of them spoke. It wasn't necessary. The expression of welcoming warmth in their eyes as they walked toward one another said everything that needed to be said, and they moved into each other's arms with an undisguised eagerness.

Their kiss eliminated all preliminaries. Morgan strained toward Jason, feeling him with her body, trying to get as close to him as their clothes would allow. It had been four days and she felt deprived of the sensations of Jason. Her tongue pushed between his lips, tasting the flavor of the inside of his mouth. She rubbed it over the sharp-edged surface of his teeth and felt the moist roughness of his tongue against her own. She took a deep breath through her nose, trying to breathe in all the various and subtle scents that made up this man whom she loved so very much.

And his intensity seemed to match hers. Running his hands up and down her spine, finally settling them around her buttocks, he pulled her tightly into him, moving his hard masculinity against her. Morgan heard a low growl emanate from the back of Jason's throat and then he pulled away from her.

Her face, starlit by love and desire, turned up to his and her voice was a misty reflection of both. "Hello."

Jason gave a low, throaty laugh. "Hello, yourself."

"Are you through working? Can you stay?"

"Yes and yes," he affirmed with considerable amusement at the rushed excitement of her words. "I even called St. Paul and told them to expect me when they see me."

"That's wonderful!"

Jason reached out his hand and ran his finger under the lace neckline of her top—just as he had done one other time, right before they had parted at the airport. The back of his finger skimmed the tops of her breasts, making her heart leap into her throat. "You sound like you missed me as much as I missed you."

She leaned unconsciously against his finger. "I did. I can't begin to tell you how much. Do the Frontenacs know you're here?"

He crooked his finger into the lace and pulled her closer. "I'm staying in one of the other cottages. There was no problem. Serge remembered me." He gave her a soft, quick kiss. "Have you eaten dinner yet?"

"No," Morgan answered guilelessly. "I was waiting for you."

They dined at the manor house, relishing the satisfaction of being together once again and laughing at the special attention that Roger gave them: Was the wine just right? Did the generous combination of chilies, garlic, shallots and tomatoes make the sauce too spicy for the firm white fish that had been marinated in lime juice? What did they have in mind for desert? Perhaps he could suggest flambéed baked bananas?

Morgan and Jason looked at one another, smiling, and then said in unison, "Why don't you join us, Roger?"

The elder Frontenac sat down, shaking his head wryly. "Please forgive me, but I so wanted this meal to be perfect for you. For days, Morgan has been going through only the motions of eating. And now, you, Jason, arrive on the scene, and suddenly she comes alive." He shrugged his shoulders unrepentantly. "I am such a romantic, you see. It is a special pleasure to me when I am able to help people enjoy this paradise that is my home."

"I understand perfectly," Morgan returned delightedly. "You see I own a shop in Minnesota that offers people 'a little bit of paradise' in the routine monotony of their lives. I know just how hard one has to work in order to bring a little whimsy into someone else's life."

Jason joined in the conversation, directing his remarks to her. "And I bet you've loved every minute of it. Because, at the same time you were pragmatically building a successful business, you have been able to indulge the fanciful side of your nature."

"You're right," she agreed, happy that he seemed to understand. "And this is my first opportunity to actually visit paradise. Before this, I've always gone to New York for my shopping trips, buying from importers."

Suddenly, for no reason, the unwanted image of David appeared before her. He had insisted on escorting her to New York the last time she had gone, saying he had to go on business anyway and they might as well go together and book into the same hotel. That way they could meet for dinner each night after their business day was through. Morgan had finally given in, too soft to hurt his feelings, but she had insisted on having her room on a floor separate from his.

"So then, is this trip for business or pleasure?" Roger asked, interrupting her thoughts.

She looked at Jason, refocusing on the present, and answered adamantly, "Strictly pleasure."

Jason left Morgan at her door that night with a simple goodnight kiss that somehow seemed perfectly right, but he was back early the next morning, looking disgustingly wide-eyed and awake.

"Ready to climb Mt. Pelee?"

"Have you lost your mind?" she mumbled, bleary-eyed and thick-tongued.

"Not that I know of," he answered bright and lively.

"Well, it's something you'd better consider—*if* you think I'm going to spend one minute of my vacation doing anything more strenuous than lifting a glass of rum punch."

"Are you always this grumpy in the morning?"

"No, not really," she apologized, stumbling back into the cottage and flopping down in a chair. "I just happen to believe that vacations are meant to be used to rest, instead of running around, enjoying yourself so much that you're exhausted by the time you get back home."

Before answering the door, Morgan had covered the filmy gown she had worn to bed with a raspberry-flowered silk wrap that Sami had presented to her on her twenty-fifth birthday, saying, "It looked like it needed you to wear it." Sami was always saying things like that, and recalling the episode made Morgan remember, "Actually, this is nothing compared to Sami's mood when she has to wake up early."

Jason had followed her in, leaving the French doors open to the easy morning breeze. "Sami?"

"I'll tell you about Sami some other time. Right now let's talk about coffee."

"Coffee?"

Morgan squinted sleep-filled eyes at Jason. "Do you always ask so many questions?"

"You're beautiful in the morning."

His deep, rich voice throbbed along Morgan's nerve endings with the intensity of an alarm going off, and she came completely awake, sighing ruefully at herself as she did so. What was she doing wasting one precious minute of their time together being even slightly grumpy?

Morgan got up and walked over to him, putting her arms around his neck and pulling his head down to hers. She kissed him softly and ardently, and Jason responded by pulling her closer, rubbing his hands over the silk that covered her body.

"You feel so damned good," he muttered thickly. "Do you have anything on underneath this robe?"

"Only a gown."

"That's too much," he growled. "I'll have to teach you to sleep with nothing against your body but me."

Jason's words sent spasms of delight quivering down her spine, and once again she marveled at the depth of response he could draw from her.

He tilted back her chin with his hand so that he could see her eyes and gave her an unasked-for explanation. "Last night, I was tired from a series of nonstop business meetings, and we were seeing each other again for the first time in four days.

Before that, we had known each other only hours. You've had one bad experience with a man. When *we* make love, I want you to be very sure that it's what you want. I'd never want you to regret it."

"Thank you," she said simply, loving him all the more.

"Right. Now why don't I get out of here so that you can get dressed? I'll meet you up at the manor house in about thirty minutes."

"Make it fifteen," Morgan replied softly.

Three

The days that followed were idyllic. In a car that Jason had rented in Fort-de-France, they toured the island at a leisurely pace, thoroughly enjoying it and each other. One day they took the coastal drive up to St. Pierre.

St. Pierre, at one time a gay and prosperous city known as the "little Paris of the West Indies," appeared to Morgan only a ghost of what it once must have been. Many years before, the city had been completely destroyed and thirty thousand people had been killed, when on May 8, 1902, in only a minute, one whole side of Mt. Pelee burst apart with a murderous eruption of fire and ash. Now there seemed to be a haunting sadness to St. Pierre and, even though it had been rebuilt, evidence of the disaster was still visible.

By mutual consent they didn't stay loı g and,

instead, got back in the car and ventured on around the island. Taking some winding, dirt roads, they came upon a palm-encircled, glistening, black sand beach near a small fishing village, where they kicked off their shoes and ate a picnic lunch Yvonne had packed for them.

Finished eating, they rested side by side on a blanket that Jason had spread, watching the fishermen far out on the water. The fishermen sailed in long, open crafts called gommiers, named for the gum trees from which the dugout hulls were made.

Morgan raised up on one elbow and shaded her eyes to get a better view, but most of them were so far out that they appeared only as dots on the flat horizon. "What do they catch?"

"Any number of types of fish, ranging from grouper to king mackerel and dolphin. What they can't eat themselves, they sell."

She turned her head to face him. "Have you been here before?"

"Once," he admitted, "but it was on business. I hate to tell you how long it's been since I've had an actual vacation."

"Well, how are you enjoying your vacation so far, Mr. Falco?" she asked teasingly.

Jason pushed her back down on the blanket. "What do you think, Miss Saunders?"

He lay over her, supporting himself with his elbows, and ran his finger inside the neckline of her cool, cotton sundress, in what was becoming a very private and erotic gesture that the two of them shared. The back of his long finger brushed sensitively across her breast, the tip of his finger reaching to the edge of the dark pink areola that ringed around her hardened nipple and which swelled toward his touch.

The start of a faint sigh of pleasure escaped through Morgan's lips, right before Jason's mouth caught the rest of it. His tongue extended into the inner depths of her mouth, savoring her sweetness, and producing gentle spirals of warmth throughout Morgan's body.

With his hand on her back, he curved her against him, using the other hand to unzip the pale blue cloth which covered her. Slowly lowering the front of the dress to her waist, he let his eyes worship the sight of her nakedness. "You are so damned beautiful," he rasped, and initiated a passion inducing exploration of her breast. Running his tongue very lightly around and around the nipple until it became diamond-hard, he turned his attention to the point itself, and began alternately sucking the nipple with his mouth and stroking across it with his tongue.

The exciting titillation made Morgan writhe beneath him with a curiously unsatisfied craving, and she heard him groan huskily at her reaction. Replacing his mouth with his hand, he kissed her lips again. Morgan's hands ran across his back, feeling the muscles bunch and roll under his shirt as he thrust against her.

The day was gloriously uninhibited and so was the way she was feeling, but raising his head, Jason pulled her dress back up on her shoulders and took a deep, shaky breath. "Morgan Saunders, you are one fantastic lady." He ran his hands through her hair, spreading the shining strands out around her head. "If sunshine were a color, it would be the color of your hair. And your eyes," he mused thoughtfully, "are as ever-changing as the sea, containing all the vibrant hues that range from blue to green."

Morgan rolled on top of him and smiled down into his face with a loving gaze, noticing how his eyes were almost black and how the gold flecks gleamed with fire. He was obviously still feeling the effects of their passion, just as she was. Nevertheless, she felt him zip up the back of her dress. "Oh yeah, well, you're not so bad yourself, Jason Falco."

Jason laughed, a roaring, joyous sound and, holding her close, began to roll them down to the sea. Like two children, they tumbled over and over, right into the water. And there in the surf of the Caribbean, the water vividly blue and translucently pure, they kissed, awash with their newfound love for one another.

Afterwards, untroubled by their sopping-wet clothes, Morgan and Jason frolicked the afternoon away, running along the beach, playing in the surf, discovering treasures discarded by the sea and, most important, sharing their unbridled happiness with only each other and, perhaps, the gulls that wheeled above them in the crystalline, afternoon sky.

Much later, feeling tired but content, they climbed in the car and started back to the Frontenac Plantation. Jason reached over and pulled Morgan closer to him. "So, you were going to tell me about someone named Sammy?"

"Sami, spelled S-a-m-i. Her full name is Samu-elina Adkinson."

"Her father obviously had made up his mind she was going to be a boy." Jason grinned. "And when she wasn't, he just added the 'i-n-a'."

"That's right. And Sami hasn't done one predictable thing since."

"How do you know her?"

"Sami and I grew up together, having both been shunted off to boarding school at an early age. My parents sent me 'to make a better person out of me,' and Sami's parents sent her to get her out of their hair."

"I find it rather hard to believe that people could actually do that to their children." Jason frowned.

"Believe it. We were both raised by strangers, but Sami got an even worse deal than I did. Everything my parents did, they did in the name of love—convoluted though it was—but Sami's parents didn't even *pretend* to be interested in her. From the time she was around three or four, her governess used to lock her in a dark, three by five closet when she 'misbehaved,' and to this day, she's afraid of the darkness and small places."

"I guess I never realized how lucky I was to be raised by two people who really cared about me," he said solemnly. "How did you manage?"

"It's a wonder we turned out as well as we did, but Sami and I had each other and we've always stuck together. When I decided to leave Boston, there was no question but that she would come with me."

"I don't suppose her parents objected."

"They were dead by that time, and Sami had

complete control of her own money. She's extremely wealthy."

"She sounds interesting."

"She is. Sami's a very special person, whom I love very much. Just because she happens to live in a slightly different manner from most people, doesn't take away from the fact that she's extremely smart and talented. Plus, she's gorgeous. She has honey-colored hair that reaches more than halfway down her back and big, beautiful golden eyes. She's also my landlady."

"Landlady! You mean she bought an apartment building?"

Morgan laughed. "Sami never does the ordinary. She bought a cavernous old warehouse over in the Lower Town District of St. Paul. My shop takes up about half of the first floor, with the other half being storage. The top floor contains our two apartments, plus a studio/workshop for Sami. My apartment is divided into rooms, but Sami has one huge room, because she doesn't like to feel closed in."

"You two live *alone*, in a *warehouse*?"

"Well, not exactly. There's Jerome."

"Jerome!"

Morgan's mirth bubbled over once again at Jason's astonishment. "Sami has a heart as big as all outdoors and she hates to be alone. Consequently, she's always bringing the strangest people home. But as it has turned out, Jerome was a real discovery. She found him selling stuffed birds at a flea market about three years ago when he was eighteen. Feeling sorry for him because there were no customers at his booth, she wandered over, bought out his entire stock of garishly painted, stuffed birds and brought both him and the birds home.

"We've made a small apartment for him in back of the storeroom. He helps out in my store part-time and goes to college. The whole arrangement has worked out very nicely. He's sort of our mascot and he helps me keep Sami out of trouble."

There was a brief silence and then Jason said, "I've got just one question: What happened to the stuffed birds?"

"Oh, well, Sami was 'into' welding about that time, and she welded a huge birdcage that stands about twelve or thirteen feet high. She put all the birds into it, in various poses and attitudes. When she's in the mood, she puts on a recording of birds chirping and changes their water."

"Don't people think that's a little strange?"

"Some do," Morgan admitted, "but Sami just tells them that stuffed birds are the only kind of birds she could ever bear to put into a cage."

Jason thought for a moment and then declared, "I'm going to like Sami!"

And Morgan, sitting quietly beside him, felt that her heart would surely burst with happiness.

The days continued just as golden as the ones that had come before, with Jason and Morgan continuing to explore the island and, in the process, learning more about each other. It was as if they knew there was no hurry—they had forever, and when they finally made love, it would be all the sweeter for their having waited until it was absolutely right.

One day they drove into Fort-de-France, enjoying the cosmopolitan bustle around them and the touch of New Orleans in the iron grillwork on the buildings. Taking full advantage of the duty-free stores lining the rues Victor Hugo and Schoelcher, each purchased a gift for the other. Jason picked out a Hermes scarf with whorls in celadon for Morgan and she bought him a handsome Dior necktie.

As they walked out of one shop, Jason slipped another small package into her hand.

"What's this?"

"Open it and find out," Jason instructed laconically.

Morgan needed no further inducement before tearing into the package. It was a purse-sized spray container of Joy. "I *love* this stuff, but I've never bought any. They advertise it as the most expensive perfume in the world!"

"I don't know about that, but I've heard it's the most romantic, and since that's how you make me feel, I wanted you to have some."

Not bothering with the fact that they were standing in the middle of the sidewalk of a busy street, Morgan threw her arms around Jason and kissed him.

"Oh, Jason," she breathed. "You're an *incredible* man."

Later, they lunched in a charming sidewalk cafe, gorging themselves on Creole cuisine and rum punch, a subtle combination of rum, sugar syrup and lime, and then strolled through La Savane, a spacious, richly landscaped square of a park near the waterfront, admiring the white marble statue of the Empress Josephine, gazing across the bay to Les Trois Ilets, her birthplace.

The sights of Martinique were engrossing, it was true, but nothing could equal the fascination Morgan and Jason had with each other. Daily, their desire grew. The sexual excitement that ran between them had been strong from the first, but as they learned more about each other, the vibrations became even more powerful. Each touch, each look, only magnified what they both realized: they wanted each other and neither one of them would be able to wait much longer.

And Morgan had the utmost faith that when it finally did happen, their coming together would be the most beautiful experience of her life. She knew it, because she knew Jason and, as much as she loved him, it simply couldn't be any other way.

The next couple of days, they stayed at the inn, enjoying the privacy of the secluded beach and the fun of trying out Serge's snorkeling equipment, discovering the wonderland that lay under the water.

One morning over coffee and some of Yvonne's delicious coconut bread, they listened to Roger talk about his plantation. "We are relatively small, compared with some of the larger plantations. Oh, not so much in land. We have more than enough." He waved a sweeping hand toward the mountains behind them. "It is just that the land has not been put to use in so many years.

"But we do not want for anything. As you have no doubt noticed, there are several large banana groves and we even maintain a small sugar cane field. There is always fish, of course, and there are numerous citrus trees about, plus mangoes and some pineapple. What we do not use for our guests' needs, we sell." He beamed, as he saw Serge walking toward them, obviously very proud of his son. "And now that Serge is back from England, we will do even better."

Serge stopped at the table. "Good morning, Morgan, Jason. I was wondering if you would like to try out my new pedal boat this afternoon. Actually, it is an old one that I have only recently renewed."

"That sounds great," Jason enthused and turned to Morgan. "What do you think?"

"It sounds like *work*, . . . but fun, I suppose." She looked at Roger and Serge. "This man is bound and determined to change my idea of vacationing."

"Are you complaining?" Jason questioned teasingly.

Looking into his brown eyes, she saw that the golden flecks were warm and tender. "Not at all," she answered softly, entirely missing the way Roger and Serge smiled at each other knowingly.

Once beyond the breakers, it turned out to be surprisingly easy.

"Piece of cake!" Morgan snapped her fingers airily.

"Easy for you to say," Jason grumbled good-naturedly. "*I'm* doing all the pedaling."

With their feet on the pedals, they were sitting side by side on a towel which they had spread along the fairly wide seat. Morgan was wearing a maillot that wrapped diagonally, forming a flattering, low V-neck, and was painted with a rainbow of pinks and lavenders. It matched the skirt which she usually wrapped around her waist and tied at the side, sarong style.

Jason's dark copper brown swimming trunks nearly matched the color of his skin. He had left the coordinating jacket on the seat beside him, along with Morgan's skirt. Picking up one of her legs and resting it across his knee, he observed, "We've both gotten a lot darker since we've been here. You've turned a light gold, but I'm afraid you've got a way to go yet before you get as brown as I am."

"You want me to get more of a tan?" Morgan inquired with pretended irritation. "You don't like me the way I am?"

Jason ran his hand casually up her leg to the inside of her thigh, causing Morgan's heartbeat to accelerate frantically. "I think you'll do," he said quite seriously, but the golden lights in his eyes were dancing.

Morgan hit out at him with a clenched fist. "*I'll do,* will I?"

Jason caught her hand easily and pulled her closer, still holding her leg across his. "Lady, if you get any better, I'll have to lock you up, and you know it."

Morgan laughed with pure delight, safe in the

knowledge that she affected him just as much as he did her. "I refuse to be locked up alone, Mr. Falco."

"Is that right?" he asked with interest and leaned forward, meeting her lips with his tongue, running the tip of it across the soft surface teasingly. His hand had begun to draw tiny designs up the tender inside of her thigh and a warmth kindled everywhere he was touching, spreading upward, matching the progress of his hand. Her open mouth fastened hungrily onto his, drinking in the delectable feast.

They had pedaled far enough out past the breakers that they didn't have to worry about being swept into shore. While they had been talking, Jason had turned the boat around so that they were drifting parallel to the beach, but far enough away so that they couldn't be seen with any clarity.

Without releasing her mouth, Jason lifted her leg and picked Morgan up, placing her across his lap so that she was straddling his body and facing him. The sensation of having her legs spread open, directly over his obviously swelling masculinity, sent a hot shaft of unadulterated desire straight through her and Morgan melted against him.

Her arms slid around his neck, as she felt him pull her breasts free of her bathing suit and chafe them against his chest, the coarse chest hair creating an exquisite friction along the tips of her breasts. "Jason!" she moaned helplessly.

He didn't answer. Instead he stabbed his tongue deep into her mouth and pulled her higher and harder against him, leaving himself room to work his fingers up into the elastic leg of her bathing suit where it had been stretched against the apex of her thigh.

The pedal boat drifted without any help, rocking Jason and Morgan gently in the cradle of the Caribbean. The flawless day sent ribbons of sunlight raying over their bodies. But neither of them noticed.

Their simple teasing had, without any real warning or effort, evolved into intensely passionate lovemaking. With Jason's fingers moving inside her, and his mouth lowering onto one distended nipple, Morgan slipped from a world made up of sun and surf, wind and sand, into one where nothing existed but hot-blooded feelings, ecstatic sensations, and an unearthly sensuality.

The sweat of their bodies mingled, making rivulets of perspiration flow down Morgan's breasts for Jason to lick off, each stroke of his tongue causing her to shudder against him. With his free hand around her buttocks, he undulated Morgan over him, causing unbearable bolts of white-hot heat to eat into her.

"Jason! Stop . . . No! Don't stop . . . don't. . . ."

"Do you want me to stop?" Jason groaned harshly against her neck. "Do you, Morgan? I can make it so good for you, if you'll only let me."

"Yes!" Morgan gasped. "Oh, Jason, for God's sake, no . . . stop . . . stop . . . before I lose my mind."

Very gently, he removed his fingers from her pulsating body, and almost tenderly, he pulled the two pieces of her bathing suit across her enlarged breasts. "I'm sorry, honey. Things got out of control before I knew what was happening. It's been hard this past week, wanting you as I do, to hold back."

"I know," Morgan murmured.

Their passion burned down, subsiding gradually and they pedaled back to shore. But they were both very much aware that the fire they shared had only been banked and that the embers were still glowing brightly.

That night, Morgan took special pains with her appearance. She had brought along an extra-terrific dress, one guaranteed to do wonderful things for her ego, and after a long, soaking bath, she slipped it on.

Diagonal stripes of amber, butterscotch and gold threaded through the silk chiffon of the knee-length frock and made Morgan feel as truly beautiful as she looked. With her hair brushed to a fine gilt and lying around her sun-tinted shoulders like a veil of gold, she pondered on the evening ahead with Jason. Their parting had been strangely stiff, and she didn't think she could bear it if their next meeting followed suit.

The fact of the matter was that, earlier in the day, while riding the shimmering swells of the Caribbean, they had passed a watershed in their relationship. Impossible to go back now, they could only go forward.

Morgan had known this time would come, so why did she have this curiously hesitant feeling about meeting Jason tonight? After all, he was the man she loved—frankly, fully, and with all of love's inherent implications.

Hearing a light tap at her door, she went to answer it. Jason, standing on her veranda, half-shadowed by the moon's silver light, white-jacketed and extremely handsome, made Morgan's heart somersault with longing. All her doubts fled. He was her love.

He held out his arms—a simple gesture, really, and one which could have a hundred meanings. But Morgan didn't need to think about it—she walked straight into them and it was the start of a night filled with perfection.

They dined at the manor house where the lights had been discreetly and intimately lowered. Candles twinkled flutteringly on every table and the sweet scent of frangipani wafted in with the night air. A local group was playing modern love songs out on the terrace, and the insistent rhythm of steel drums underlay each tune, managing to instill the songs with the primitive beat of the surrounding jungle and making the night throb with a torrid undercurrent.

Morgan wasn't sure what she ate or drank. Her awareness was concentrated solely on Jason. His eyes had turned black, shooting flames of gold across the small table and into her soul, and when he stood up and offered her his hand, she took it. Out on the terrace, she went into his arms once more, this time to dance in the rawly electric atmosphere of the tropical night.

Their bodies were communicating without either of them speaking. They moved together in an instinctive way—a way of sharing, without words, the thousand and one things they wanted to say to each other. And Morgan heard what his body was saying.

Everywhere he was touching her had suddenly become a focal point of sensitivity. Her breasts were resting against his chest and even through their clothes, a warm languorous heat was winding, starting from her nipples, continuing into her breasts and spreading inwardly right on through her body.

Jason's arm was placed low on her back, clasping her tightly, pressing her pelvis into his, and making a new and separate weakness advance slowly down into her lower limbs. His other hand was holding hers, and even there, heat was radiating up her arm, expanding to different parts of her, parts she hadn't been aware of before tonight.

Then he took the hand he had been holding and placed it around his neck, his hand joining the one on her hips, unobtrusively caressing her softly rounded bottom. The pads of her fingers where they touched his neck burned and they stroked up the strong column, to behind his ear, lingering in the small hollow they found there. In response, Jason pulled her even tighter against the hardened arch of his thighs, and Morgan felt her body ignite into a raging fire.

Overhead, the moon was spinning webs of silver and the night cast out threads of magic, weaving them in and around the two of them, entangling them in its net of desire. Morgan raised her head and looked at Jason. Her vision blurred, her throat clogged, she whispered, "If you don't make love to me soon, I think I may die."

Jason became instantly still, looking deeply into

the blue-green depths of her eyes that were dazed by an unbounded desire for him. Taking her hand, he led her off the terrace and through the garden, which teemed with red and purple bougainvillaea vines, pink gliricidia trees, red ginger and porcelain rose, all in various degrees of bloom. The large, highly colored leaves of the anthurium mingled with the orange and purple flowers of the bird of paradise plant and marked their way down the path to her cottage.

Entering it, they didn't bother shutting the French doors or even switching on the light. Instead, they turned to each other in a fury of need and kissed with a deep hunger, clinging and straining, until Morgan couldn't have stood without Jason holding her. She didn't notice when he unzipped her dress, but she felt it as it whispered down her legs, settling around her ankles. Then he was lifting her, carrying her to the bed and laying her down.

Stopping only long enough to undress himself, Jason joined her. Morgan could feel the trembling in her body as Jason slowly ran his hand over her, eliminating the rest of her undergarments as he did.

The velvet of the night winged into the open doors, carrying a gossamer breeze on wings of softness and, with only moonlight banding their bodies, Jason and Morgan made beautiful love to one another.

Morgan, using her tongue to taste the virile flavor of Jason, ran the tip of it around his nipple, enjoying the groan he gave and the way he clutched at her. Lying on top of him, she undulated farther down his body, loving the abrasive tingles she created, taking tiny, delicate nips of him as she went.

"God, woman! Where did you ever learn this witchery!" he gasped hoarsely. Gripping her tightly, Jason rolled over on top of her.

"I think I learned it the minute I opened my eyes and saw you," she responded, gasping in turn when she felt him mouth the taut peak of her breast and commence sucking, and his hand move between her legs, caressing.

Stark passion boiled through Morgan's blood, such as she had never known, such as she had never expected. "Now!" she cried. "Please . . . now . . . *Jason!*"

He entered her in one clean stroke and a pleasure streaked through her so intense that she called his name again and again. There was no awkwardness, as there sometimes is with people who are making love for the first time. Rather, their bodies moved in perfect oneness, synchro nized to the finest degree. Their overpowering need for one another swiftly became ungovernable, taking them higher and higher, their movements quickening.

Jets of fiery liquid began to course through Morgan with an urgency that suddenly became a molten pressure, so volcanic in its force that it burst apart within her, erupting with a dynamic intensity equal to the explosion that once caused lava to flood out of Mt. Pelee. Afterwards, damp and glowing, she slept in Jason's arms, completely fulfilled and utterly content. Before the morning's sun rose, they made love again.

There was all too little time left of their vacation, but they continued to make the most of the days left, sightseeing, playing and, most of all, loving.

On the last day of their vacation, they drove to the other side of the island. There they discovered a village where a few of the women were engaged in batiking, the method of dyeing designs on cloth by coating with removable wax the parts not to be dyed, and Morgan made arrangements to have some of the cloth shipped to her store.

They returned via La Trace, zigzagging their way through the rain forest, and decided to stop. Walking hand in hand through the enchanted forest filled with ferns—tiny ones, knee-high ones and giant tree ferns—they marveled at the fairy-land of green. However, nothing could compete for long with their intoxication at the presence of one another, and Jason soon turned to Morgan.

He nuzzled her neck and inhaled deeply. "You smell so good. Are you wearing the perfume I bought you?"

"Ummmm . . ." she acknowledged dreamily. "You know, I've never seen anything like this. There just aren't enough words to describe this place properly."

Jason took her fully into his arms. "I feel the same way, only about you. Your beauty defies all known words. You make me want to invent new ones."

Running her hands around his neck, Morgan gazed adoringly at him. "You realize, don't you, that what we've found on this paradise of an island is something very special."

Jason's mouth quirked wryly. "With you, Morgan, I find I don't think a whole lot. I just feel."

"What are you feeling now?"

Her whispered question wrested a deep growl from Jason. "I feel like laying you down in this bower of green and making love to you until your cries of ecstasy echo across the forest."

The strength and power of her love for Jason overcame her, and Morgan's fingers began to move restively over his chest, stopping to unbutton his shirt. "Do it . . . please, Jason, do it."

His hands went purposefully to the knot behind her neck, releasing it, and the halter top Morgan was wearing fell to her waist. Reaching behind her, he untied the final knot and the top fell to the ground.

Jason's grip on her arms was as strong as steel, but there was a definite gentleness to his actions as he held her, dropping them together onto the carpet of ferns. Morgan peeled her shorts off and lay waiting eagerly while Jason took the remainder of his clothes off.

The glade they were in was interspersed with wild orchids, fragile pink in color, and was laced with sunshine that rivaled the golden sparks glimmering in Jason's eyes. His mouth covered hers in a kiss that was as old as time, yet as new as their love for one another, and Morgan's tongue mated with his, receiving and giving. There was nothing reserved in the way her body curved against him; she wanted to be possessed by him and her murmured words of desire told him so, but Jason was in no hurry.

He moved his attention to the side of her neck where he grazed up to her ear, tenderly exploring that delicate orifice to his complete satisfaction, before nibbling unhurriedly back down her neck and over to her breastbone. With the moist sorcery of his tongue, Jason drew a deliberately precise line between her breasts and then traced under them, where he paused to nip the sensitive underside of the weighted fullness.

Morgan heard the sound of an impassioned moan and realized it had come from her, as Jason continued his journey around her breast, completing a full circle with his tongue, and then switched to the other breast, to begin again making maddeningly methodical circles with his mouth, around and around her breast, coming closer and closer to the rigid tip, until Morgan didn't think she would be able to stand it if he didn't reach his destination soon.

"Jason . . . oh, Jason . . ."

"Darling," he breathed onto the heated surface of her skin. "We've got all the time in the world."

His mouth stopped beside her nipple, and Morgan's stomach tightened with expectation. Closing over the throbbing point with his teeth, Jason gently moved it back and forth, causing small ripples of pressure to commence deep within her. His hand came up to support the breast, squeezing it, urging the nipple further into his mouth.

Morgan put her hands on Jason's shoulders, sinking her fingers into the muscled flesh. Her hips arched erotically upward. She wanted Jason *now*. She didn't want to wait. She wasn't sure she could. But Jason's mouth went to her other breast, using it with an alternate pressure and friction to intensify the gales of pleasure that blew in waves through her body.

Her fingers threaded through the dark gloss of his hair and attempted to bring him up to her. Instead, Jason's head moved lower, over the silky expanse of her stomach . . . and even lower, his tongue and hands seeking, probing and memorizing the geography of her body. Morgan felt his fingers push into her buttocks and raise her so that he could have better access to the inside of her thighs. Then, rubbing his tongue into the highly sensitive feminine folds located there, Jason brought Morgan to a never-before-reached fever pitch of passion. Her whole body quivered with an ache so intense it threatened to consume her if it wasn't relieved soon.

"Please . . . oh please," she pleaded almost incoherently.

Jason raised and plunged into Morgan in one bold motion, entirely filling her with himself. Their overwhelming desire for one another took over, making them forget time and place. Yet lying under a jungle canopy of green, in a tropical woodland, the two of them were in strange and wonderful fellowship with their primeval environment. Natural forces prevailed around and in them, and Morgan dug her nails into Jason, dragging them the length of his back, as their mutual cries of ultimate release shattered the peace of the forest.

Quiet returned to the rain forest and eventually to them. Resting beside Jason, Morgan breathed happily. "I don't think there has ever been a place or a day such as this."

"Don't ever forget," Jason whispered back.

Four

Still heady with happiness from their vacation, Jason and Morgan deplaned into the crowded Minneapolis-St. Paul International Airport late the next afternoon. Despite the throng of milling people, it was not difficult for Morgan to spot Sami.

Wearing a purple Cossack top with fuchsia and jade flowers embroidered around the high collar and down the asymmetrical placket, over a tight pair of jeans that she had stuffed into navy-colored, high-heeled cowboy boots, Sami was standing in the middle of what looked like a group of religious cult members. A belt with an enormous free-form gold buckle measured her narrow waist and a Navy pea coat was draped casually over one arm. Sami, as usual, looked magnificent.

"Sami!" Morgan yelled, and grabbing Jason's

hand, started to push their way through the crowd.
Sami's long blond hair swished around her shoulders as she turned, waved and started toward
them. Observing how the crowd parted and then
turned to stare at her beautiful friend, Morgan
grinned. Sami could part the Red Sea if she put
her mind to it.

But then Sami's arms were around her in a
tight, crushing hug and her words came tumbling out in a jumble of excitement. "I'm so glad
you're back! I thought you'd never get here. How
was Martinique . . . and the plane ride? I didn't
tell you, but I had a little talk with the pilot and
he promised to fly carefully."

"Should I ask what *you* promised *him*?"

"Nothing more than to have dinner with him!"

"I guess it was worth it then, because we didn't
crash. Of course, I'm not at all sure I would have
noticed even if we had." Morgan held her friend at
arm's length, laughing at the amazed expression
on her face. "I see nothing has changed here."
She nodded over Sami's shoulder toward the religious group that had followed. Despite the frigid
weather outside, they were all dressed uniformly
in green tunics, with open sandals on their bare
feet, and wore identical bland expressions and
lengths of long hair, making it hard to tell what
sex they were. "You haven't invited them for dinner have you?"

Sami glanced behind her, giving the group a
graceful shrug of dismissal. "Oh, no. I was just
trying to find out where they get their tunics.
Turns out they're issued to them, just like in the

army, and you can't get one unless you join their organization."

"It's the wrong color green for you, anyway," Morgan consoled. "Listen, there's someone I want you to meet." She pulled Sami around to face Jason, who had been watching the two equally stunning young women with quiet amusement.

Sami's great golden eyes sparkled with comprehension and genuine delight. "Morgan! You found him!" She extended her hand to Jason, clasping his large hand in her small one. "I knew it, I just *knew* it! You don't have to tell me who *you* are! You're 'Tall, Dark and Handsome,' right?"

"Sami, behave yourself!" Morgan laughed. "This is Jason Falco."

"Of course he is." Sami was still beaming her smug satisfaction at being right up into Jason's face, and she hadn't let go of his hand. "Did you two have a simply wonderful affair?"

"Sami!"

"Yes, we did," Jason answered with unembarrassed ease that made Morgan love him all the more, "and as a matter of fact, we still are. What's more, I doubt very much if our affair will ever end."

"Oh, *you're marvelous!*" Sami informed him gleefully and finally let go of his hand to turn back toward Morgan and demand, "Didn't I tell you?"

"She'll never let me hear the end of this, you know," Morgan groaned wearily to a somewhat puzzled Jason. "Don't ask me how, but she *predicted* you!"

Jason laughed and drew Morgan into his arms, giving her a light kiss on the cheek. "Sami, however you did it, I'll be indebted to you for the rest of my life."

Sami shrugged modestly. "Nothing to it—just a little black magic."

"Is she serious?" Jason asked Morgan.

"It's hard to say. I haven't seen her in two weeks."

"Hey!" A plaintive voice intruded through the din. "I just fought off the whole defensive line of the Minnesota Vikings, a mean-looking traffic cop and two nuns for a parking place. Don't I get a kiss?"

"Jerome!" Morgan rushed over to the tall, lanky young man with the sandy-colored hair and planted a big kiss on his smiling lips. "How have you been?"

"Great. And I don't have to ask about you. I can see. Martinique must have agreed with you—I've never seen you look more beautiful."

"And this is why," Sami informed him triumphantly, breaking in on their conversation and dragging Jason over to them. "Jerome, this is Jason Falco. Jason this is Jerome Mailer. He lives with us."

"More or less," Jerome amended and extended his hand toward Jason, his pale blue eyes twinkling behind square-shaped, tortoise-rimmed glasses.

"Morgan told me all about you," Jason said, "and it's a pleasure to meet you. Incidentally, I like your jacket."

Jerome glanced down at the chocolate brown World War II pilot's jacket he wore. "Thanks. Sami brought it home one day after an afternoon of scavenging in one of the thrift shops she frequents."

"I'll have to send her out shopping for me sometime."

"I'll be glad to," Sami chimed in, immediately getting caught up in the idea. "With your dark complexion, you'd be devastating in a long Moroccan caftan . . . maybe gold," she mused, looking him over thoroughly.

"I'll think about it," Jason promised dubiously, once more reaching out a long arm to Morgan and bringing her back to his side. "I enjoyed meeting you both, but right now I'm afraid I've got to get to the office."

"Do you have to?" Sami questioned with disappointment. "I was hoping we could all have dinner together."

"I'm afraid so. I was supposed to be back over a week ago, and if I stay away any longer, they're liable to put out a missing persons bulletin on me."

Jerome spoke up. "In that case, why don't Sami and I go get the car, Morgan, and you can meet us at the curb with your luggage?"

"Fine." Morgan was grateful for the additional few minutes alone with Jason. "And by the way, Sami," she called over her shoulder. "You better contribute to that group's cause or they might just follow us home. They seem to have taken to you."

After retrieving their bags, Jason and Morgan made their way slowly toward the entrance, prolonging their inevitable separation.

"You know where Paddy's and Company is, don't you?" Jason asked, naming an Irish bar-restaurant located about halfway between their two apartments. "Why don't we meet there around seven tomorrow evening?"

"Okay," Morgan agreed readily, but then added ruefully, "I think the next twenty-four hours will be among the longest I've ever spent."

Jason didn't reply, but the force of his parting kiss showed Morgan that he felt the same way.

The next morning, Morgan relaxed at the window of her second-story apartment, wrapped in a warm robe and drinking a cup of coffee. From where she was standing she could see the Mississippi, frozen solid in mottled gray and white designs for the winter, and the stark outlines of iced-encased tree limbs, struggling against the harsh elements to survive until the spring.

Everything was the same, yet everything was different, Morgan reflected with happiness. Now she knew Jason Falco lived in St. Paul, and that knowledge made her automatically look at her surroundings differently. Had he noticed how brightly the sun glinted off the snow this morning, she wondered? What was he doing at this exact moment? Was he looking out his window and thinking of her? Morgan wanted to run to the phone and call to ask him, but she resisted. Jason had said seven tonight and she would wait.

Showered and dressed, Morgan was just about to make her way down to the shop when the phone rang. She answered with eagerness, thinking that it might be Jason. "Hello?"

"Morgan?"

It was David DeWitt. She had completely forgotten about him! Swallowing her disappointment, she answered brightly, "David. How nice to hear from you. How did you know I was home?"

"Are you kidding? I've been marking the days off my calendar, one by one. " His voice lowered. "I've missed you terribly and I'm dying to see you."

David was so nice, Morgan thought, and she hated to hurt him; but she realized that she had let their relationship drift casually for entirely too long, believing it was the "kind" thing to do. However, now she had only one choice: she had to break off with him, once and for all. With this in mind, Morgan said, "I-I'd like to see you, too, David."

"You would? Great! How about lunch today?"

He sounded like a little boy looking forward to a special treat and Morgan's burden of guilt felt all the heavier; nevertheless, she answered firmly, "That would be perfect. I'm anxious to talk to you."

"Good. By the way, my brother is back in town, and I want you two to meet. I've been telling him all about you, so don't let me down."

"I won't," she responded distractedly. "Goodbye, David." Her mind was already on how best to explain to him that she would not be seeing him at all anymore. She would be cruel if she had to. The important thing, now, was her relationship with Jason. Nothing could be permitted to hinder it.

David's office was in the DeWitt Building, one of the new hi-rises in the downtown area, not too far from the warehouse. As Morgan entered the building, she gave little notice to her surroundings. It was true she had never been to David's office before—all she knew was that it was the head-quarters for his family's vast business holdings—but it didn't matter, because she didn't plan ever to be here again.

Punching the elevator button for the next to the top floor, Morgan unconsciously straightened her shoulders, dreading what was to come. She hated the thought of hurting anyone, but unfortunately, she had to do it. And she could comfort herself with the knowledge that in a few hours she would be able to see Jason again.

Just the mere thought of Jason sent a warm flush of feeling surging through her, and she stepped off the elevator looking very beautiful. The powder pink of her soft wool dress harmonized beautifully with the rose-beige of her cashmere coat and the brown of her leather boots. The cold wind had whipped color into her cheeks and snowflakes into her hair, causing her to glow and glisten with the winter day.

David met her with his office door opened wide, his happiness at seeing her very apparent in his uncomplicated, nice-looking face. "Morgan, darling!" His arms enfolded her even before she had a chance to back away. "How I've missed you." He pulled back slightly, laughing, his voice intimate. "Before I get you alone and show you just *how much* I've missed you, I want you to meet my brother. Come on in."

Morgan walked into a well-lit, spacious office and came to an abrupt halt at the sight of the man sitting behind the desk. "Jason!" Her heartbeat accelerated with the unexpected joy of seeing the man she loved sooner than she had expected. "What are you doing here? This is a wonderful surprise."

David had followed her in. "You mean you two already know one another?"

"Jason?" Morgan's voice dropped to a tentative level. He was sitting silent and unmoving, with his three-piece, pin-striped suit making him appear extremely dark and formidable. His brown eyes were almost black, but it wasn't with the passion Morgan was used to seeing in them. All of a sudden it dawned on her that Jason Falco was very, very angry—frighteningly so.

David put his arm around Morgan and cuddled her limp body against him. "This is great, Morgan. I hadn't realized that you knew Jay. I've been wanting to get the three of us together for months now, but somehow I could never get all of our schedules to dovetail."

Jason wasn't talking, so she turned to David. "I don't understand. You mean *Jason* is your brother?"

"My half-brother, hence our two different last names. We have the same mother, with Jay being the older by eight years."

There had really been nothing to warn her. Even though the two brothers shared similar coloring, they looked nothing alike; David was slightly shorter, with a softer look about him.

"You call him Jay?" Morgan repeated the name dazedly. She was in shock. Not only with the news that Jason was David's brother, but with the fact that Jason was incredibly angry.

"It's what our family has always called him. When his father died, he left Jason a fortune and a slew of businesses that were held for him in trust until he became old enough to take control. My father, in effect, raised Jason as his own, and when he died, he left me his businesses, but with Jason being in overall control of everything and with a sizable interest. We've consolidated our businesses, dividing up the responsibilities, yet Jason remains the head." David looked at Morgan, a little perplexed. "But I've told you all of this before, haven't I?"

"Maybe. I don't know." Morgan couldn't take her eyes off Jason. He seemed so cold, so distant. And now it was very apparent that it was *she* that he was furious at. What could have happened in less than twenty-four hours to cause his anger?

"Well, if you didn't know that Jay was my brother, how did you meet him?"

"Martinique." She could only manage the one word, but it said everything.

"Oh, sure. How stupid of me. I had forgotten that you two would be down there at the same time. Jay's schedule is usually so hectic, it's hard for me to keep up with him. It must have slipped my mind that he'd be down there to check up on the newest DeWitt House at the same time that you would be there on a holiday. What a coincidence!"

"Coincidence," Morgan echoed hollowly, but her mind was racing. What was wrong with Jason? Why was he looking at her as if she were a complete stranger? She wanted to go to him and throw her arms around him, but the look of controlled rage on his face told her very clearly that she would not be welcomed.

It was as if, when she had walked into David's office, she had crossed the border into a foreign country, and nothing could make any sense without a translator. Yet, there didn't seem to be anyone qualified to act as one—except Jason.

David pulled her closer to him and kissed her cold cheek, obviously blind in his enthusiasm to Morgan's confusion and Jason's fury. "I couldn't be happier that you two have already gotten to know one another. Jay and I have always been close, and since one day soon, I plan for you and me to be married—Jay! What the? . . ."

Jason had bolted from his seat and stalked out. Not waiting to hear anymore, he had passed his brother and Morgan without saying a word.

"I'm sorry, Morgan," David began, "I don't understand—"

"David!" she interrupted with urgency. "Where is Jason's office?"

"Why, it's upstairs—wait a minute!" He grabbed her arm as she started out the door. "What's going on here? I think I deserve an explanation."

Morgan had no time to be tactful. "I'm in love with Jason. I had no idea he was your brother, David, but to be perfectly frank, I'm not sure it would have made any difference if I had known. We met on the flight down to Martinique and fell in love . . . or at least I fell in love with him, and I thought he returned the feeling."

"I don't understand. I thought that you and I—"

"You don't understand, because you've never *listened* to me, David. I've tried to tell you before, in as nice a way as I knew how, that I'm not in love with you and that I could *never* be in love with you!"

"But I thought—"

"You *thought*, David. You wanted it so much that you refused to believe that it couldn't happen. I fully accept the blame. I should have been firmer. It was just that I didn't want to hurt you and I thought that with time you would see for yourself what I had been trying to tell you. But after I met Jason, I knew there was no more time left. I came here today to break off with you, once and for all. I never in a million years connected your beloved 'Jay' with the man I fell in love with on my vacation."

Morgan could see that the facts were sinking in with David. She was hurting him, but she couldn't help it. She had to find Jason and explain.

Once more she started out the door and once more David pulled her back, his voice colder now, angrier. "You mean to tell me that after months of our dating, after months of my hoping that you would marry me, after *months* of my respecting your wish not to make love, you went to bed with my brother after knowing him only a matter of *days*?"

Morgan's voice gentled with compassion. "That's exactly what I mean, David, but you must believe me when I say, I never meant to cause you pain. I'm sorry." He made no effort to stop her this time, and she walked out the door.

Finding Jason's office on the top floor with no problem, she marched right past the startled secretary and flung open his door. "Jason!"

Jason turned slowly from his rigid stance at the window. He was someone Morgan could no longer say with any certainty that she knew, for this coldly withdrawn man bore little resemblance to the warmly demonstrative lover she had known so intimately in Martinique.

"What do you want?" His words were like ice.

Morgan closed the door behind her and advanced toward him. "I want to know what the problem is."

"Problem!" he mocked sarcastically, sitting down at his desk so that the width of it stretched formally between them. "Why, whatever do you mean, Morgan? Just because I return home and find that the woman I've just spent days making passionate love with is my brother's girlfriend—why should you think that there's a problem?"

"Look. I realize it's a little awkward, but—"

"Awkward!" he shouted. "Where do you get your nerve, Morgan, with your sunshine beauty and your jewel-colored eyes, to come in here and tell me that this situation is a 'little awkward'?"

"Jason," she pleaded, "listen to me."

"No, Morgan." The sharpness of his voice was cutting her to ribbons. "I listened to you on the plane when you told me that there was no one waiting for you back here. I'm not listening to you anymore."

"It's true that David and I dated—"

"Dated! My brother is crazy about you. He thinks that the two of you are going to get *married*."

"He might have wished that before, Jason, but now I've explained to him about us."

"Oh, good! Tell me, Morgan, did you leave anything out? Like the fact that I made love to you so often that I know you inside and out?"

"Jason . . ." She went weak, just thinking of the times they had been together. "I told him that we slept together—"

"And I suppose you're going to ask me to believe that David took it well and wished us happy."

"Not exactly, but—"

"You're damned-well right—not exactly!" Jason's fist slammed down on his desk. "I can only imagine the hell he's going through."

"He'll get over it, Jason."

"I'm going to make sure of that, sweetheart," he sneered. "I would guess that your type of scheming woman is only too easy to get over."

Scheming woman? This *couldn't* be happening! They had returned to St. Paul incalculably happy, yet as soon as he found out that she and David had dated, Jason had lowered some sort of iron curtain between them. Morgan ran her hand through her hair in bewilderment. "I never misled him *or* you, please believe me."

"Believe you!" He came up out of his chair with such deadly intent, Morgan wouldn't have been surprised if he had meant to strangle her. Instead, he made an obvious effort to get himself under control. Resting his clenched fists on the desk, he lowered his head and took several deep breaths.

Watching him, Morgan felt like he *was* killing her, slowly and by inches. How could one misunderstanding cause such havoc and pain? She wasn't sure that she completely understood everything, but there had to be a way to make things right again. There just *had* to be.

However, when Jason finally raised his head and looked at her, his voice was ominously quiet and solidly under control, and he made it quite clear that there was no hope.

"David is my brother. I've loved and protected him since the day he was born, and no woman"—he ran a scathing glance over her—"is going to come between us. When his father, the man who raised me with care and love, died, he entrusted David and his inheritance to me. David and I share a tie and a bond that someone like you could never understand. My loyalty is, and will always remain, with David." He paused for a moment with sadistic timing, making her wait before he delivered the final blow. "Now get out of here. I never want to see you again."

Morgan turned automatically and moved silently to the door, like a robot without a heart. Her hand was on the doorknob, when she heard him add, "And Morgan. If you go anywhere near David again, I'll make you so sorry, you'll wish that you had never been born."

Daylight had gone; moonlight had not yet come. There was only twilight, that peculiar state of suspension, where there is neither darkness nor light. In her apartment, Morgan sat very still and alone, willing her mind not to work. She didn't know how long she had been sitting there, hours probably. It didn't matter. She had discovered that nothing mattered as long as the blessed numbness continued—that deadened feeling that had encased her mind the moment she had left Jason's office.

Yet, the sensationless void where she had retreated didn't seem to be working as well as it had been. Vague emotions had begun to swirl around the edges of her consciousness, trying to intrude into the empty calm of her mind. Morgan put a hand against each side of her head, attempting to push away the thoughts.

"Morgan! For God's sake, I've been beating on your door. Didn't you hear me?"

Taking her hands away from her head, Morgan looked up through the dim light into Sami's worried face. "I guess not."

"What are you doing sitting in the dark?" Sami moved around the room, her compulsion for light making her switch on lamps. "Jerome said he saw you come up here hours ago, and I got worried when you didn't call and check on me like you usually do. That was the whole idea of your having the phone installed for me in the first place, wasn't it?"

"What's the use? You never have it plugged in anyway."

Morgan's wooden tone brought Sami back to her. "You know I hate phones," she murmured absently, her golden eyes intent on her friend's pale face. Dropping down on her knees, Sami picked up one of Morgan's cold hands, chaffing it. "What is it, love? What's wrong? Tell me."

Sami's soft, caring questions were the thing that finally broke through to Morgan as nothing else could have. She leaned forward, throwing her arms around Sami, and started to cry. "He hates me, Sami. He hates me!"

"Who hates you?"

"Jason. He's furious at me."

"That's impossible, Morgan."

"I know, but it's true," she sobbed. "He was so cold, like someone I had never met. He said he never wanted to see me again."

"That doesn't make any sense. The man I met at the airport was very much in love with you, Morgan. You're obviously wrong and crying is not going to help us figure out why." Sami pulled away, smiling gently. "If it would, I'd join you. God knows, I've cried on your shoulder enough times. Where are your tissues?"

"Over there," Morgan sniffed, pointing in an indeterminate direction.

Sami was back in less than a minute. Thrusting a handful of tissues in Morgan's face, she ordered, "Blow."

And Morgan did, reflecting ruefully that for all of Sami's eccentricities, she could be maddeningly practical at times.

"Okay"—Sami sank cross-legged to the floor, her sapphire silk caftan billowing out around her— "what's happened?"

"It's David." Morgan gestured vaguely through the air with her wad of scrunched-up tissues.

"David? I thought we were talking about Jason."

"Would you believe it, Sami? They're brothers!"

"Brothers? How? Where? When?"

"You'll have to check with their mother on that one," Morgan replied humorlessly.

"I don't understand. Why didn't they tell you?"

"Oh, it's all been a crazy mix-up." Morgan got up and paced to the window, an incipient anger directing her movements. "I went to David's office today to break off with him, to convince him that there could never be anything between us, and there sat Jason behind David's desk. It turns out that David's beloved half-brother 'Jay,' the one he has been wanting me to meet for months, is none other than Jason."

"Good grief!" Sami began to twist a long blond curl around and around her finger. "Well, I can see where this might make things a little awkward—"

"That's what I said," Morgan reported glumly.

"—but surely, with you and Jason loving each other as you do, it can be overcome and worked out."

"I thought so, too." Her voice was becoming firmer. Her own brand of wrath, rage and fury was beginning to vie for position within her. "We found something beautiful and rare on Martinique. How could he have forgotten it so soon?"

"Maybe he hasn't," Sami reasoned, untwisting the curl and starting on another one. "But maybe for some reason he feels as if he's been betrayed by you."

"Why? I haven't done anything wrong."

"Of course you haven't!" Sami was nothing if not loyal to her friends.

"And I tried to explain to him about David."

"I don't know what to tell you, love. He obviously feels that his support must go to his brother."

"I can understand that. I really can. A love be-

tween brothers is very special, and from what I
can gather, theirs is more so than usual."

"Something like you and I have developed—a
love and friendship that's been forged through
years of pain and happiness?"

"That's right, but what I need to get across to
him is that what he and I share will not threaten
their relationship. I admire Jason for his basic
integrity regarding David. He takes his responsibilities and loyalties very seriously, and strangely
enough, it's a trait that he and I share. I would
never want to interfere with or change that. How
could I, loving him as I do? It's part of what goes
into making him such an incredible man. But I
happen to have a strong belief that we had something unique and precious going for us, and that
we can hold onto it without me coming between
the two of them."

"Yet, inadvertently, it seems you've done just
that—come between them."

"And no one feels worse than I do about it,
believe me. Whether Jason realizes it or not, I
have a deep compassion for the hurt that David is
feeling at the moment. However, what Jason's got
to know is that this will all lead to a vicious fallout.
He can't be happy. I can't be happy. And David
would have been even more unhappy if he and I
had continued seeing each other, with him eventually realizing that I could never love him as he
had hoped. Or, on the other side of the coin,
when he learned that he was the cause of the rift
between Jason and me. I now realize what a huge
mistake it was to continue seeing David at all!"

"It could be that you and Jason had such a

whirlwind affair that he feels he can't trust what he learned about you. But any way you look at it, and for whatever reason, Jason is just not thinking straight at the moment."

Morgan hit her fist into the palm of her other hand, new color and resolution in her face. "Well, that's just too damned bad, because I'm not going to let Jason get away with ruining what we had between us because of some *stupid* misunderstanding. He can't just turn his back on this situation."

"Now you're talking!" Sami clapped her hands together in excitement. "What are you going to do?"

"I don't know exactly, but that man loves me and I love him and somehow I'm going to get him to admit it."

Sami jumped up. "I've got just the thing to help you. I'll be right back."

She stared sightlessly at Sami's retreating back, already beginning to plan. Morgan had a history of going after what she wanted—and she was going after Jason.

It was true that Jason had never said he loved her. But then, words had always seemed so unnecessary between them—their bodies had said it all. In spite of everything, there was only thing to consider: Morgan knew she loved him more than ever. He *must* feel the same way.

Her thoughts were interrupted by Sami bursting back into the room. "Here it is—all you ever wanted to know, but were too indifferent to ask!"

"What?" Morgan looked blankly down at the book that Sami had thrust into her hand.

"It's a book I bought the other day called, *159 Ways To Seduce A Man.*"

"What in the world are you doing with a book like this?" Morgan asked, flipping through the pages. "You're still a virgin!"

"I wanted to be ready when the right man comes along," Sami responded with indisputable logic.

"Ha! That'll be the day! Men have been hanging around you since you were a little girl, and you've never shown the slightest bit of interest one way or the other."

"You'll see. There's someone out there just for me, and he'll come along one of these days."

"Well, I want to be there when he does, because you probably won't recognize him when you do see him."

"You're wrong, Morgan. I'll know him in an instant."

"Could I interest you in David?" Morgan questioned hopefully.

"No way. I'll find my own, thank you very much."

"Here's hoping you find one less thickheaded than the one I found," Morgan muttered and stopped at one of the pages that had a particularly interesting illustration on it. She looked at it one way, then she turned it upside down and looked at it the other way. "There is no way that this can be done," she finally pronounced. "No one could possibly get into that position."

"Let me see." Sami grabbed the book out of her hands, half closing her eyes to get a different perspective, then turning the book sideways for another view. "Maybe, maybe not. But I bet it sure would be fun to find out."

Taking the book out of Sami's hand, Morgan threw it over her shoulder with reckless self-confidence. "I don't need that. With as much love as I feel for Jason, I don't need *anything* else."

Sami looked at her and burst out laughing. "You and I are quite a pair, Morgan—the original poor little rich girls. In different ways, we've searched all our lives for love . . . fighting against the odds . . . daring to try to be happy."

"Yeah, but you know what?" Morgan grinned softly back. "We've never given up. Heaven knows we've had plenty of discouragement, but we've never let anyone beat us yet! And I'm not about to let Jason Falco break my heart!" Morgan put her arms around Sami and hugged her close. "We're going to be okay, Sami. I've found my dream of happiness and I'm not going to let him go. Someday you'll find yours, too."

Five

Thinking that even though Jason wouldn't listen to her explanation in person he might take the time to read a letter, Morgan sat down and proceeded to write her heart out. She explained as best she could how stubborn David had been when she had tried to break off with him, and how she had decided to adopt a neutral route—giving him no encouragement, while at the same time doing her best not to hurt him—until the time David could come to the same conclusion she had. The conclusion being, of course, that it would never work out between them, because they simply didn't love each other.

Morgan gave Jason a few days to read the letter and to cool down, hoping against hope that he would call. But he didn't, and as Morgan saw it, the ball was in her court. She had tried reasoning with his mind. Now maybe it was time to try something else. She made her move.

One afternoon at precisely 4:55 P.M. Morgan assumed her most businesslike voice and placed a call to Jason's office.

"Mr. Falco's office."

Staring across the room at a hanging plant, she crossed her fingers and said the first name that came into her head. "Yes. This is Ms. Ivy Basket. I wonder if it would be possible to see Mr. Falco this afternoon?"

"I'm sorry, Ms. Basket, but Mr. Falco can't see anyone else today. He plans to get away from the office promptly at 5:30. Perhaps tomorrow sometime?"

"Thank you." Morgan smiled her pleasure into the phone at the indiscreet secretary. "I'll give you a call."

Congratulating herself on her success thus far, Morgan put Step Two of her strategy into action. By her calculations, there was a certain spot that Jason had to drive by, in order to get from his office to his apartment, and that was where she headed. Accurately judging the late afternoon traffic, Morgan arrived at the spot on the dot of 5:28.

Pulling her car to the side of the road and turning off the ignition, she got out and raised the hood, looking at the contents of her car's engine with considerable interest and almost no knowledge. However, a few months back, she had had some trouble with the car. The culprit had turned out to be a loose battery terminal wire, and her friendly neighborhood mechanic had instructed her to be careful of it. Now her fingers went immediately and unerringly to the wire and loosened it imperceptibly. Complacently assured that everything was going according to plan, she set her sights on the traffic and waited.

Fifteen minutes later she was still waiting and her confidence was beginning to waver. A freezing rain had commenced falling and darkness was descending rapidly. Morgan had counted on Jason being able to see her clearly. She had also counted on not having to wait over five minutes for him.

Standing beside her car, practically out on the road, so that Jason couldn't possibly miss her, depressing thoughts began to enter Morgan's head. What if he hadn't planned on going to his apartment after he left the office? She had just assumed he would. What if he had taken another route? It was entirely possible. What if something had come up at the last minute, and he hadn't been able to leave the office when he had hoped? It now seemed likely that something must have detained him. Or what if he had left five minutes early?

"Fine time for you to think of these things now, dummy!" Morgan railed at herself, trying desperately not to think of what her mother would say if she could see her now. Her mother had always stressed the importance of being a lady, and Morgan had a terrible feeling that what she was about to do had *nothing* to do with being a lady. On the other hand, maybe there were two definitions of the word.

Rows of impersonal headlights bounced off her

shivering figure, one after another. Feeling wet and cold clear through to her skin, Morgan rubbed her hands up and down her arms and tried to quiet the chattering of her teeth. "Jason Falco, where are you?"

Just then, a car slowed down and pulled off the road a little ahead of her. Excitement raised inside Morgan, and she started toward the dark form of the car. But a strange man rolled down the window and shouted back at her, "Is there anything I can do, lady?"

Morgan stopped short and called out, trying to sound convincing, "No, thanks anyway, but I'm expecting help any minute now."

The man waved and drove off, leaving Morgan staring gloomily after the departing red tail lights. That was the second false alarm. One other man had also stopped to offer help. Glancing at her watch to see that it was nearly six, she gnawed on her lip, trying to figure out what to do, but mostly trying to keep her teeth from hitting together.

Damn Jason! Who had asked him to sit down beside her on the plane, anyway? Heaven knew she hadn't, and now she would most probably die from pneumonia because he had.

Another set of headlights hit her, passed, then the car braked and pulled off the road. She heard a car door slam, and then, almost immediately, the figure of Jason was towering above her in an unmistakable rage.

Rage? Morgan thought. She had hoped for concern; at the least, she had expected curiosity; but, she decided practically, she would settle for the rage—just as long as he had *finally* shown up.

"I thought it was you! Damn it, Morgan, it's sleeting. What in the hell are you doing standing out here?"

Sleeting? Morgan looked around herself in amazement. She had become so numb with the cold that she hadn't even noticed when the rain had turned to sleet.

"Well, hi, Jason. Gosh! What a lucky break for me that you happened along. I was beginning to think that no one was going to stop and offer me help."

"Don't you realize how dangerous it is out here? You are standing so close to the road. If any of these passing cars were to lose control, they could run right over you." He stopped his ranting to glare at her. "What's the problem anyway?" His glance went past her to the raised hood. "Did your car break down? What's wrong with it?"

"I really don't know. It just quit running." Morgan shrugged helplessly, trying to bat her eyes, but finding that they must have frozen into a permanent squinting position.

"That could be anything from the electrical system to an empty gas tank," he grumbled. "Damn it! I don't even have a flashlight, and I sure as hell don't feel like standing out here getting wet. Come on. I'll take you to your apartment, and you can call a garage from there."

"Are—are you sure that it won't be too much trouble?" she questioned with what she hoped sounded like feminine timidity.

"It will be nothing *but* trouble, but I don't see any way out of it," he growled.

Inside the warmth of his car, Morgan found that she really *couldn't* stop shaking. It had been part of Step Three to fake being cold, but now it took no effort on her part to ask through chattering teeth, "Jason, won't we g-get to your apartment before we reach mine?"

"So?" He wasn't going to give an inch.

"C-c-couldn't we just stop there for a few minutes so that I could get dry. I'm s-soaked to my skin and f-freezing."

"It shouldn't be that much farther to your place," he argued stonily, "and the car heater is on."

"But traffic has gotten much slower since the w-weather has worsened. It'll take at least fifteen more minutes to get to the warehouse, and I k-know that I'll get sick if I have to wait that long."

Silence was the only thing that greeted her tremulous statement. She prodded. "Isn't your apartment just up in the next b-block?"

More silence.

"Jason, please?" Morgan beseeched and then sneezed with absolutely brilliant timing, almost as if on cue.

A curse split suddenly through the warm air in the car. "*All right, Morgan.* But you're only staying long enough to get dry and warm. Is that understood?"

"Why, of course, Jason."

Unfortunately, once at his apartment, Jason's temperament didn't improve. Morgan didn't even have time to take in the comfortable elegance of the main room, or the masculine appeal of his bedroom, before Jason shoved a glass of whiskey in her hand and directed curtly, "The bathroom is straight through there. Throw your clothes out when you get them off and I'll put them in the dryer."

"You want me to take my clothes off?" Morgan screwed her face into a befuddled expression that she hoped Jason would find appealing and funny; she finally managed to bat her eyes successfully, red-rimmed though they must be.

"What else do you suggest?" Jason was almost gnashing his teeth. "By the time you've finished with your shower, your clothes should be just about dry. Use my robe, wait in the bedroom and I'll bring you the clothes when they're ready."

Despite her genuine discomfort, Morgan could hardly keep from laughing. Poor Jason. She had banked on him not being able to pass her on the road once he had seen that she needed help, and then not to let her suffer when he realized she might get sick. She had been entirely right. So far, everything was going perfectly and Step Four was about to begin.

Morgan entered the black, gold and chrome of his bathroom and stripped off her clothes, not bothering to shut the door. Tossing them invitingly through the opening, she turned on the shower as hot as she could stand it and got in, making a face, as she heard the bathroom door slam decisively shut. Jason Falco was definitely a hard nut to crack.

Morgan knew she couldn't stay in the shower long if his dryer was as fast as he had indicated.

Nevertheless, she took a moment to luxuriate in the warmth of the steam billowing around her and to enjoy the feel of the hot water streaming down her body, slowly defrosting every cell.

Until she had met Jason, Morgan had never been particularly aware of her body, one way or the other. Now she discovered that she was very conscious of how her body responded to the touch and texture of things around it—most particularly to the touch and texture of Jason.

But knowing that she couldn't afford to day-dream too long, she lathered her hair with a rich shampoo she had discovered on a conveniently-placed shelf, quickly rinsed it and got out of the shower.

Finding Jason's bathrobe with no trouble, she tried it on with a grimace of distaste. There was too much of it. It just wouldn't do. Shrugging out of it, she seized instead a fresh black velour towel, deciding it would fit in much better with her plan, and wrapped it loosely around herself. She left her hair wet, combed back and lying shiningly over her bare shoulders, and her skin glowed trans-lucently against the vivid black velvet of the towel. Not bad, Morgan decided, saluting herself in the mirror with the glass of whiskey, and downed the contents, reflecting ruefully that, since meeting Jason, she had certainly changed from being an almost complete teetotaler.

Walking silently on bare feet into the living room, she paused for a moment, locating Jason. He was slouched on a stool with his forearms resting on the bar. Staring broodingly into a glass of some-thing, he appeared far away in thought.

Yet he must have sensed her presence, for suddenly he whirled around, stopping the motion of the stool when he saw her. His face turned even stonier, if that were possible. He seemed as cold as the ice storm that was raging outside, and Morgan wondered despairingly if she would ever be able to thaw him.

Resting his body back against the bar in an arrogant attitude of ease, so that he was practically lying on the edge of the stool with his legs apart, Jason watched insolently, as Morgan sauntered leisurely across the room to him, the sinuous motion of her hips thrusting alluringly against the towel.

"Why aren't you wearing the bathrobe?" he demanded gruffly.

"I found it," she answered truthfully, "but it just didn't fit. It wrapped around me about three times and dragged the floor." She turned away from his probing stare and began wandering around the room, curious to see the kind of things with which Jason surrounded himself.

Jason was a rich man, yet he lived in a relatively small apartment, expensively and tastefully furnished though it was. There could be all kinds of reasons. The most obvious one was that he was a single man who was constantly on the go and who didn't have a lot of free time to spend in a home.

Picking up items that caught her fancy, Morgan examined them, pondering on their possible history in Jason's life, and then put each one down, feeling the towel slip a little more with every movement of her body. In one corner of the room she found a heavily cut crystal bowl in a prominent position on an antique etagére and containing a large assortment of richly colored marbles. Fingering one of them, Morgan looked back at Jason, trying to envision a man who had perhaps started collecting marbles when he was a boy and had continued the practice into adulthood. She saw a muscle working at the side of his cheek and his eyes were nearly black, but at this point it was hard to tell whether it was with anger or passion.

Moving on, she saw the beige-colored envelope addressed to Jason from her, opened and lying on the mantle. That answered one of her questions. He had received the letter and read it. Her hands went next to a book lying face down on a chair. The leather binding felt worn, as if it had been read many times. She turned it over and saw that it was a collection of Shakespeare's plays. Funny . . . she had the same volume at her apartment.

Progressing on, she discovered an expensive and complicated set of stereo components. He liked music, but that she had known. Any man who could dance as well as he, had to have a natural feeling for music of all kinds.

She couldn't stand it anymore. There was too much silence in the room. She had to speak to him. "Do you know what I was thinking while I was taking my shower?"—Morgan didn't expect or wait for an answer—"I was thinking of the rain forest where we made love, that last day we were on the island. Do you remember? The glade where we made love was cool, but we created our own heat." She hesitated and peered at him from under her lashes, trying to gauge his reaction to her attempt at ensnaring him in their memories.

"Didn't we make a corner of heaven for our-selves there? I've never experienced anything like it before . . . have you?"

His eyes were silently monitoring her random progress about the room, alertly observant to her every gesture. She stopped at his chess set and picked up the king, idly rubbing the brass finish. She knew she felt warmly damp and smelled freshly of his personal soap. She could feel his rising need of her clear across the room. So *why* wasn't he saying anything? Couldn't he tell how much she loved him?

She put the chess piece down and picked up the queen, studying it thoughtfully. "You have to realize that for years I thought I was frigid. Yet even before you first kissed me, I felt, in a strange, almost mystical sense, that my life was about to begin—in you." Morgan turned to look fully at Jason. "And there has never been anything so right in this world as the moment when we finally made love. I could easily have died of the pleasure you gave me—*you*, Jason, only you can make me feel that way."

Morgan began to walk toward him, trailing her fingers over the satiny wood of a table she passed.

Jason came to his feet with an apparent unwill-ingness, almost in a trancelike state, as if his actions were quite beyond his control.

She stopped before him. There was so much inside her that she wanted to say, but she didn't know how or which words to utter next. It seemed such a crucial moment! Tears filled her eyes. Oh

God, she thought, in self-derision, here she was in Jason's apartment, half naked, with his full attention, and she was about to make a complete fool of herself by crying.

She reached for a napkin that lay on the bar to wipe the tears away, but the motion caused the towel to slip from around her body and down to the floor. Morgan froze for a split second in time, seeing now the blaze of desire that lit the darkness of Jason's eyes. But it was the only thing that touched Morgan, because Jason didn't move. They were both being held captive in the grip of the hotly powerful emotions running between them.

Jason's eyes never lowered from hers. Nevertheless, the tears finally spilled over, making poignant paths of wetness down her cheeks. There was only one thing she could say, and she said it. "I love you, Jason."

With a deep groan, Jason reached for her, pulling her into him. Their lips met in an eternity of a kiss, and they hung tightly on to one another with a fierceness of need that spoke more clearly of the truth of Morgan's statements than anything she could have said. It went on and on until, at last, he pushed her away so that his shaky fingers could get to his shirt buttons.

Morgan's hands encircled the back of his head, and her mouth came down on his throat, moving inside the shirt collar to the base and licking at the spot directly over his pounding pulse. She could feel the back of his hands graze against the bareness of her breasts as he worked on the buttons of his shirt, and a fresh joy of the promise of his love sprang up in her.

"It seems like forever since we were together in Martinique," she murmured into his skin, her lips moving across his throat and up behind his ear, where her teeth took hold of his earlobe, chewing gently.

At the same time, her hands began massaging his neck, easing the tenseness of his strongly corded muscles. Jason thrust his shirt off impatiently and brought her back to him, his hands caressing the tips of her breasts that were exquisitely pointed with desire.

"Touch me, Morgan," Jason demanded raggedly. He sat back down, pulling her between his legs, and his hands went compulsively under her buttocks, pulling her more forcefully up into the incredible virile strength of him, where his hips began nudging against her in a wanton demonstration of his passion.

She met his movements. Raising on tiptoe she pushed down against him, beginning an up and down motion, with the strength of his arms supporting her. "I feel empty without you, Jason. It's an ache deep inside of me that I can't get rid of without your help. Only *you* can fill me."

Jason's tongue curled inside her slightly parted mouth, tracing a path across the ridges of her teeth and up under the velvet edge of her lips.

"I need you so, Jason," she breathed, her breasts rubbing incessantly on his chest, her lips moving over his mouth. "*We need each other*, and you can't say it isn't true."

Morgan drew back, looking deeply into Jason's

eyes and the fire she saw there seared through her, heating her blood to an almost unbearable degree. "Can you?"

"No." The answer seemed to be torn painfully from him. "No, damn you, I can't."

His mouth attacked hers, grinding her lips against her teeth until she tasted her own blood. Or maybe it was his. Morgan didn't know or care. Jason loved her, he wanted her—she was sure of it.

His tongue was inside her mouth, pillaging the moist interior, yet it still wasn't enough. Jason pulled her down to the floor with him. The carpet felt soft under her nakedness, and Jason felt hard as he ground his hips against her.

"God, Morgan! I want you so badly."

His mouth fastened on her nipple with near violent hunger and she curved her back, thrusting her breast deeper into his mouth. "Now, please now. Don't make me wait. I can't." It must have been her final plea, but to her astonishment, he rolled abruptly away from her. "Jason?" she cried, feeling like a part of her had just left.

"Damn you to hell, Morgan! Why did I let that happen?" His chest was rising and falling with the great heaves of his effort to get himself under control. He threw one arm across his eyes.

Morgan raised and reached out to stroke a hand over his chest. "Because you can't forget how it was between us any more than I can."

"I'll tell you what else I can't forget," he gritted, throwing her arm away. "I can't forget how my brother is suffering because of the two-timing little bitch you are."

"Jason, I tried to explain—"

In one quick motion Jason was on his feet. Scooping up her forgotten towel, he hurled it at her. "You can't talk fast enough, Morgan, to make me forget the disgust I feel for you. Now, get up. I'll bring your clothes to the bedroom, and I'll call you a cab, but I want you dressed and *out* of here in five minutes."

Morgan walked slowly back to the bedroom in a daze of incomprehension, an awful pain of pure misery eating her insides away. She knew that Jason had been as aroused and had wanted to make love as much as she.

In her state of hurt confusion, Morgan also knew one other thing—she wasn't going to give up. That man loved her, and she was going to make him admit it or die trying.

Jason reached the bedroom before her with his hands full of her clothes. Tossing them contemptuously on the bed, he turned and stamped out, barking a reminder over his shoulders, "Five minutes, Morgan."

Dressed with two minutes to spare, she stood in the middle of the room, her gaze sweeping longingly around it, seeking the solace that Jason's personal belongings seemed to bring her. The jacket Jason had been wearing was lying across the back of a chair. Morgan picked it up and held it close. She had never in her entire life felt more vulnerable. His rejection had hurt terribly, all the more so because she couldn't understand it.

She hugged the coat close to her body, trying to draw some comfort from the warmth of it, but a hard mass dug into her. Opening the jacket, she found an appointment book. Morgan looked at it with misgivings. After all, invading someone's privacy was naturally abhorrent to her, but perhaps if she scanned through it, she would be able to discover something, some clue that might help her.

And she did, finding what she read there to be very interesting. Two nights from now, if the book was correct, Jason was supposed to have dinner with someone named Melinda at Paddy's and Company.

The rat! That was the restaurant where the two of them had been going to meet the night after they had gotten back from Martinique. And here he was, just a few days later, meeting another woman. The man obviously had no scruples. A mischievous smile split Morgan's tear-stained face. Well, then, *neither did she!*

Carefully replacing the appointment book, she looked around the room once more and then quietly left the apartment.

"So then you'll do it?" Morgan asked eagerly.

"Of course he'll do it," Sami affirmed spiritedly.

The person on whom the speculation rested viewed the two young women resignedly. "Just what exactly does it entail?"

"Honestly, Jerome!" Sami protested. "That's the lawyer coming out in you. Always wanting to know the fine print."

"Oh yeah? Well, it'll be a certified miracle if I ever make it into law school the way I keep having to interrupt my education to help you two out of the messes you somehow manage to get yourself into." He threw his hands up in the air. "I really don't understand how you got along without me all those years."

"Interrupt your education! That's a big laugh when you consider how, at first, I had to practically drag you down to the university and sign you up myself."

Jerome shrugged impassively. "Once I found out the university was coeducational, I decided it was worth getting involved. Actually, I rather like it now. My favorite time is between classes, when I get to walk from building to building."

Morgan's mouth quirked into a wry grin, as she listened to Sami and Jerome's teasing banter. The truth was that Jerome was a serious student with one of the highest averages in his class. At the moment, there were quite a few law schools jumping at the chance to get him. And as far as Sami's involvement went, everyone present, including Jerome, knew that his dream of an education couldn't have become a reality without Sami's help, both financially and emotionally.

The three friends were lounging in Sami's staggeringly huge, one-room apartment before a free standing fireplace that served both as a place of warmth and as a divider between her living room and bedroom.

"Will you both just hush up?" Morgan asked, focusing her attention on Jerome. "As to what the evening will entail, don't worry about a thing. Just leave it all up to me."

"When you say 'don't worry about a thing,' " he drawled, "that's the time I start worrying."

"You know," Sami said, pursing her lips and again going off on another tangent, "I would never have thought that Jason would be the type of man to go out with another woman."

"You only met him one time, Sami," Jerome reminded her dryly.

"But you know what a good judge of character I am. No." She tossed her head, causing her blond hair to ripple down her back in honey-colored waves. "There's got to be more to this than meets the eye. Any man who refuses to see Morgan again has got to be either crazy or . . . I've *got* it! This Melinda must be a high-priced call girl."

"Sami!"

"Well, honestly, Jerome. Can you think of any other reason why Jason would go out with another woman so soon after he's had an affair with Morgan?"

A lopsided grin tugged at Jerome's mouth. "Your logic escapes me, but I'm almost afraid to ask."

"That's okay. I'll be glad to explain it." The slightly raised gesture of her hand toward him spoke of grand condescension. "Jason obviously found Morgan so good in bed that—"

"Sami!" This time the protest came from Morgan, but heedless of her friend's embarrassment, Sami forged sublimely on.

"—that he needs a woman, and instead of wanting to get emotionally involved so soon after the experience of their totally perfect love, he decided to just *pay* for it."

Morgan looked at Jerome and shook her head wryly. "I wonder why I don't feel comforted by that thought?"

"If it's not that," Sami persisted, "then she must be the classic 'other woman'—the type that can smell his wounds and has decided to move in for the kill. In other words, a real hard-shelled bitch."

Morgan cleared her throat loudly. "Can we please get back to the subject at hand?"

Sami looked at her in astonishment. "Which is?"

"Which is, Jerome accompanying me to Paddy's and Company tomorrow night."

"But I thought that was all settled."

"Not exactly," Jerome broke in. "I'll do it, of course, but I'd just like a few more details—such as, am I going to have to kill, maim or maybe seduce anybody? You know, just general stuff like that."

"Don't be ridiculous. All you have to do is watch me and follow my lead."

"You don't have a plan yet, do you?"

"Not really."

Six

Paddy's and Company was a popular gathering place for the young "movers and shakers" of the city and on this particular night, the bar was packed to capacity. Since it was always crowded, Morgan knew that one needed to have reservations well in advance in order to get seated for dinner at a reasonable hour, and it was for that very reason that she hadn't bothered making any.

"Are you sure he's coming?" Jerome asked, not for the first time.

"That's what his appointment book said, unless 'Melinda' changed his mind for him."

"Yeah? They could have decided to skip dinner and get right to the main course."

"That's not funny!"

"Oh, come on. You know I'm just kidding. How about another drink?"

"No thanks. That's how I got into this mess in the first place—downing a double Scotch at the airport."

"If you say so, but I'd be willing to wager my tuition for next semester that you're not sorry."

"You'd win." Morgan smiled reluctantly and looked at her watch for the umpteenth time. From their carefully selected position in the bar, Morgan knew that they would be able to see anyone who entered or left the restaurant.

Just then, the hostess passed in front of the opening to the bar, leading a well-dressed brunette and . . . Jason toward the back of the restaurant, where rows of intimate booths were lined around the dance floor. Each booth had heavy red velvet curtains that the diners could either let down for complete privacy or leave tied back for a view of the dance floor.

"There they are. I hope they leave the curtains tied back so that I can tell which booth they're in."

"Don't worry. We can always bribe a waiter." Jerome studied Morgan meditatively. "How long are you going to give them?"

"I don't know." Morgan stared anxiously at the now empty doorway. "Let's give them a few minutes to get settled."

But the longer Morgan waited, the more nervous she became. And worse luck, the girl that Jason was with didn't look anything like a prostitute—or a hard-shelled bitch either! Morgan honestly didn't have any clear idea what she was going to do. She only knew that she would do just about *anything* to break up Jason's evening with the gorgeous brunette he was with.

"Okay." Morgan suddenly slammed her hand down on the table. "That's long enough. Let's go."

Holding tightly onto Jerome's hand, she led the way toward the back room, then stopped at the doorway to survey the scene. At first she didn't see them and panicked in case they were behind one of the many closed curtains.

"Over there," Jerome whispered in her ear. "The second booth from the right."

"I'll kill him," Morgan muttered, as she finally saw Jason and his date. They were sitting across from one another, the booth curtains opened, and Jason had one of the girl's hands in his, talking earnestly to her.

Quickly crossing the room, Morgan slid into the booth on Jason's side, before he had a chance to realize what was happening. "Jason! Good heavens. Imagine seeing you here!"

Jerome had followed a little more slowly and slid in beside the girl. Morgan forced her voice to a sparkling brightness. "You don't mind if we join you, do you? We were just about to be seated for dinner when we noticed you. I told Jerome, 'Jerome,' I said, 'there's Jason. Wouldn't it be fun to join him for dinner.' " Morgan petitioned Jerome, "Didn't I say that, Jerome?"

"That's what you said, all right."

Morgan looked at Melinda. "This is Jerome Mailer— Jason already knows him—and I'm Morgan Saunders." Morgan extended her hand toward the self-possessed young woman, so that she had to take her hand away from Jason's. "Of course, Jason knows me, too, but then I'm sure he's told you all about how we met on the plane to Martinique."

"How do you do," the woman responded politely, but her beautiful brown eyes were definitely not friendly. "I'm Melinda Johnson."

"Melinda! What a *sweet* name," Morgan gushed. "It sort of conjures up images of ruffles and bows, doesn't it?" Even as Morgan said the words, she cringed. She knew they sounded catty, yet she couldn't seem to help herself. This woman was absolutely gorgeous, *and* she was on a date with Jason. In Morgan's book, the latter was enough to make Melinda an automatic rival.

"Morgan!" Jason spoke for the first time.

"Yes, Jason?" She scooted right up against him and smiled her most seductive smile.

"Would you folks like a drink before dinner, this evening?" The question came from their waiter, who had arrived opportunely, thus saving Morgan from hearing what Jason had been about to say. Actually, she didn't need to hear it. She could see from his face that he was coldly furious. But then, Morgan reflected philosophically, he seemed to stay that way lately.

"Oh, that sounds great." Morgan took over. "What would you like to drink, Melinda?"

"I'll have a strawberry daiquiri."

"A strawberry daiquiri," Morgan repeated, managing to infuse the words with a slight interest and, at the same time, a faint disdain. She turned to the waiter. "I'll have a Scotch. No water. No ice."

After the men had given their orders, an uncomfortable silence fell among the four people, leaving it to Jason to say, "Morgan . . . Melinda and I have some things to talk about this evening."

"Oh, that's perfectly all right. We don't mind. Do we Jerome?"

"Nope."

"Don't you worry about us." Morgan patted Jason's knee, receiving immense enjoyment from the involuntary flinch he gave. "You two just go ahead and talk about whatever it is you need to talk about, and we'll just sit here and be quiet as two little mice. We won't be bored at all. Isn't that right, Jerome?"

"That's right, Morgan."

Morgan took a moment to look narrowly at Jerome, but then switched her gaze to the woman beside him. "And speaking of not being bored, our holiday in Martinique was simply marvelous, wasn't it Jason?" Morgan again lay her hand on Jason's knee, this time keeping it there. However, after a sideways peek at his face, she very prudently shifted her eyes back to Melinda, deciding not to take too many chances at once.

Continuing her monologue, while at the same time moving her hand in unhurried, small spirals up Jason's leg, she confided to the other woman. "The place was a virtual paradise for lovers."

Melinda looked down her nose at Morgan. "Really?"

The woman had a definite attitude problem, Morgan decided. "Oh, yes. The days were a seduction in themselves, but the nights. Well, words fail me when I think about the moonlit Caribbean nights we spent there. . . ." Jason's leg had gone quite tense under her hand. She glanced quickly at him and saw a man who had ceased to breathe.

When her hand had nearly reached the top of his leg, she paused there for a couple of seconds, pressing her fingers into the hard flesh beneath the material of his slacks. Then she lightly dragged her nails back down his thigh to his knee, where she started the stroking all over again—only this time even slower.

"And then there was the day we took the ferry across Fort-de-France bay and drove around the southern coast of the island to see the H.M.S. Diamond Rock. I tell you, Melinda, it was amazing. This *hard* rock, just lying there in the afternoon sunshine." Morgan reached the top of Jason's thigh and stopped there once more, dallying, giving him ample reason to wonder whether she was going to go any farther.

Evidently Jason decided not to take the risk. Even though there wasn't much room between him and the wall, he shifted over a little, managing, without being too obvious, to break their contact. There wasn't much he could do without creating a scene, and Morgan had an intuitive feeling that he didn't want to do that in front of Melinda.

Undaunted, Morgan lowered her voice to a huskily erotic pitch. "It made my heart beat faster just to think of how *engorged* in history that rock is—standing so *erect*, five hundred seventy-five feet high."

As she spoke, her fingers began walking across the booth seat toward Jason. However, he must have been keeping an eye out, for his hand came down on top of hers with, what she privately felt was, an unnecessary force. Nevertheless, it was better than not being touched by him at all, and her hand went limp under his.

It was impossible to miss the immediate surge of electricity that seemed to jump from his hand to hers upon contact. And, Morgan reasoned, if she was feeling it, so was he. Jason started to pull away, apparently relieved that she was offering no resistance to him, but Morgan quickly turned her hand over and linked her fingers securely through his. Now he couldn't get away.

A mini tug of war ensued under the table, with Jason trying to jerk his hand away, and Morgan pulling it back, as she continued speaking.

"It's *stimulating* just to think of how *tightly* those British sailors *heeeeld* it"—the word "held" was more forcefully emphasized than Morgan had intended, because Jason had chosen that moment to give a particularly vicious tug—"for eighteen months during the Napoleonic Wars."

Looking at Jerome, Morgan saw that his cheeks were flushed and he was intently studying the ceiling, but Melinda seemed to be hanging on Morgan's every word, torn between trying to figure out what she was talking about and being worried about the expression on Jason's face.

"England has actually commissioned it as a British sloop of war, and I think it's inspiring how that rock has become a symbol of their patriotism." Morgan leveled her blue-green eyes straight into Melinda's brown ones, and her voice took on a strong note of conviction. "I admire the *courage* and the *passion* of those men to defend that which is *theirs*!"

With the hand that Morgan didn't have control of, Jason was holding his glass of whiskey so tightly that his knuckles were turning white. He raised his glass unsteadily to his lips and took a long swig.

"And the rain forest. Well, what can I say about the rain forest . . . except perhaps that it was the *climax* of our whole trip."

Jason spewed his drink back into his glass. Grabbing her hand, he pushed her out of the booth with the impetus of his body. "Excuse us," he bit out to Melinda and Jerome. "Morgan and I are going to dance."

Once out on the dance floor, Jason took her stiffly in his arms. "You're not being very damned subtle, Morgan."

"I wasn't trying to be."

"Well, I for one would be extremely interested to know what you *are* trying to do."

"I'm attempting to get you to remember what it was like between us, so that you'll realize—"

"*Remember!* Why would I want to remember what amounted to nothing more than a cheap affair with an equally cheap woman, who can no doubt be had by just about anyone who wants her. After all," he drawled cruelly, "if you recall, *I* had no trouble whatsoever in picking you up."

A pain stabbed deep into Morgan's heart. One part of her brain was screaming out in despair that Jason could say such a thing—but the other part of her brain was saying, "Don't give up. He's lashing out at you in blind anger, in an attempt to convince himself of what he's saying, as well as you."

"That was no common pick-up, Jason! What we had between us was uncommonly and utterly extraordinary, and I won't let you pretend otherwise."

Morgan didn't know whether it was her words or the hurt tone of her voice that got through to Jason. Whatever it was, he relented. "You're right, and I apologize. It's just that you make me *so crazy!* Why can't you just give up and leave me alone?"

Jason's hold on her relaxed somewhat and she managed to burrow against him, relishing the instant response she felt leap from his body. "You know what the trouble with us is?"

"What?" he asked hoarsely, apparently curious despite himself.

"We're *not* alone. I miss the sound of your voice, the touch of your hands, the deepness of your laugh." She paused, looking up at him wistfully. "We did have fun together, didn't we, Jason?"

"Yes," he admitted grudgingly.

"It's important for two people who are in love to be able to have fun together. But there are other things, too. I want you near me once more, to feel you against me—"

"Morgan, for God's sake! Stop it!" He gave her a jerk to emphasize what he was saying, but he had jerked her *closer* to him, although that was obviously not what he had intended.

On some level, she *must* be reaching him. Maybe at the moment it was only his body, but somewhere deep inside, Jason had to know that he loved her. She just had to get him to admit it, and Morgan prayed with everything she had in her that very soon now, she would be successful.

"Take Melinda home and come to me," she whispered softly into his ear, trying to keep the shakiness out of her voice. "Remember that perfect night when we first made love in my cottage? There was only the moon, the sweet fragrance of frangipani and the two of us. It can be that way again, Jason. I'll turn out all the lamps in my apartment. I have some frangipani scented candles, and I'll light them. We can drink rum punch as we did on the island and discuss this problem, work it out and find a solution. Then we can make love the whole night through; we can talk and laugh and make love till the sun rises, and in the early daylight if you want." Lightly brushing against Jason, she reveled at the sound of his sharply indrawn breath, as she felt him fight for composure.

Regardless of whether they were angry at each other, there was always this fierce heat that ran between them. Surely, nothing could be as important as their love for one another. Jason *must* see that!

"I have no intention of taking Melinda home," he groaned huskily, holding her tightly to him. "She is something you'll never be, Morgan. She doesn't lie or cheat the people who care about her."

"Melinda doesn't turn you on like I do, Jason. I bet she's never lain beneath you in a rain forest—"

"Shut up, Morgan!"

"You've *got* to understand. There's no one else but you. Please believe me." Her words were laced with quiet desperation.

"My brother doesn't lie."

"Where *is* David?" she asked, upset with herself that she hadn't thought of it before. "Let's go to him, talk this problem out between the three of us. Whatever misunderstandings there are, I'm sure they can be cleared up."

"David is someplace where you can't get hold of him, and he's going to stay there until I think he's over you."

"I want to talk to him, Jason. We need to get things straightened out, once and for all, so that you and I can get on with our life together."

Jason pushed her away from him. His face had gone pale and his teeth were clenched. "Pay attention to me, Morgan, because I want to make myself perfectly clear. *Stay away* from David and *stay away* from me. I don't want to see you or have anything to do with you ever again. Martinique was a mistake, but it won't be repeated."

He started off the dance floor, but Morgan grabbed him, catching him off balance and pulling him back to her. People around them had begun to stare, but Morgan spoke loud enough for only Jason to hear. "Now it's your turn to pay attention to me, Jason Falco. I love you, and sooner or later you're going to have to admit that you love me, too. Call me, any time of the day or night, and I'll come to you, wherever you are. *I'll be waiting.* I want you to remember that, to think about it when you're lying in bed at night by yourself, and you're aching so badly for me that you can't sleep. Think about it—and *remember* it."

She strode past him to the booth and grabbed her coat and purse. "Come on, Jerome, we're going."

Jason had come up behind her, and, not even bothering to say goodnight to Melinda, Morgan turned to look at him one more time. Her eyes were a brilliant blue-green and they flashed her desire for him, unmistakably and openly. Jason swallowed convulsively, not able to look away, and then Morgan turned, walked out of the back room, down the long hallway and out into the cool blast of the night air.

"Wait up, Morgan," Jerome called. "For heaven sakes, put your coat on or you'll freeze to death."

Morgan stopped. "Lord help me. You're right, and it would be just like Jason to bring Melinda to my funeral."

"Yeah, and you'd be 'just too dead' to do anything about it."

Putting her coat on, she sighed morosely, "Either I'm losing my sense of humor, or your jokes are getting worse, Jerome."

"I'm only trying to cheer you up."

"I know and I appreciate it, too, but I'm absolutely miserable! I can't *believe* what I just did. I don't know who was the most surprised or embarrassed—me, Jason or Melinda."

"I think I'd have to say Jason. You didn't look at him that often—"

"I didn't dare."

"—but it appeared suspiciously as if he were blushing a time or two."

"I thought I could do something like that and not feel any shame or remorse afterwards, but now I'm not so sure. It's just that I get so mad at that dumb, stupid, stubborn, self-righteous man."

"I gather you're no better off than before."

Morgan paused and then smiled with sudden insight, a little more sure of herself. "That's where you're wrong. I'm like a sculptor who spends all of his time chipping patiently away on a material of his choice to form a work of art. That's what I'm doing. I'm slowly chiseling away the stone from around Jason. Soon I'll reach his heart, and when that happens, I will have re-created something awesomely beautiful—Jason's and my love for one another."

Walking slowly toward her car, Morgan noticed that they were passing Jason's car. "Wait a minute!"

"Now what?"

"Just a little insurance to make sure that Jason thinks of me while he's taking the beauteous Melinda home." She delved through her purse to get the atomizer of perfume Jason had bought for her. Luckily he hadn't locked his car door. Opening it, she sprayed a generous amount of the perfume into every corner of the car, knowing that the porous leather of the upholstery would absorb the scent and that it would be a long time before the smell of her would be completely gone from his car—and his mind.

During the next few days, Morgan found herself again questioning her actions. Even though she had had the satisfaction of breaking up Jason's date, she couldn't seem to keep away the guilt she felt at the *way* she had done it. And being an honest and candid person, she finally admitted to herself that maybe it was time for an apology.

Picking up the phone to call him, she decided upon an open and direct approach.

"Jason Falco's office."

"This is Morgan Saunders. I was wondering if it would be possible to see Mr. Falco this afternoon?"

"No, Ms. Saunders, I'm sorry, but it isn't."

"Well, then, can I speak with him?"

"I'm afraid not. You see, he didn't come in today."

"He's out of town?"

"No. I'm sorry to say he came down with a cold and has been feeling really terrible. He left early yesterday afternoon."

"You mean he's home sick?"

"That's right. Can I set up an appointment for you later in the week?"

"No. Thank you anyway." Morgan hung up and mulled over this new piece of information. Jason had been working too hard. She had noticed the lines of tiredness in his face at Paddy's and Company, but at the time she had been so upset with him for being with another woman that she hadn't given it much thought.

Now, however, her heart went out to him. She wanted to go to him, to take care of him, to make him feel better. So she did exactly that.

It was almost dark by the time she reached Jason's apartment. Since both her hands were full, she kicked on his door. He didn't answer, so she kicked a little harder. Still no answer. Visions of him lying unconscious raced through her head. She kicked loud enough to raise the dead, plus most of their neighbors, and this time he did answer.

Opening the door, he yelled, "Stop that infernal noise!"

Clutching her packages, Morgan pushed her way past him and then turned to observe worriedly.

"You look awful." He appeared feverish, with red and watery eyes and a nose that was swollen from blowing it too much. "And you need more clothes on," she scolded gently, viewing the bare legs and feet that were sticking out from under his bathrobe.

"I wasn't exactly expecting company," he snapped sarcastically. "What in the hell are you doing here, Morgan?"

"I heard you were sick, and I wanted to help you."

"Then leave."

"I stopped off at a restaurant and picked up some good homemade chicken soup," she told him, hoping to tempt him. "Sami sent an herbal tea concoction for you, and Jerome sent the makings for several hot toddys."

"You're wrong—" he started to say.

"You know, you're right," Morgan considered thoughtfully, kicking the door shut. "I think it was Sami who sent the hot toddy makings and Jerome who sent the herbal tea."

"Morgan!"

"You shouldn't be standing here, Jason," she admonished with real concern. "Come on, let me help you into bed."

"That's what you've been trying to do ever since we got back from Martinique," his words were muffled behind the pillowcase he held up to his nose. "But you're not going to be successful."

"My intentions are strictly honorable," Morgan promised gravely, as she began pushing him in the direction of the bedroom. "Your virtue is safe."

But once there, Morgan gave a cry of alarm. "Jason, this place is a mess. And that bed. You can't get any real rest in that. The sheets are dirty and the covers are thrown every which way."

"I alternate between being either too hot or too cold," he mumbled from behind the pillowcase. "I can't seem to get comfortable. I ache all over. I don't feel good."

"Look, while I change the sheets, why don't you go take a hot shower. It'll make you feel better and at the same time perhaps open up your stuffy head."

"I don't want to." He sounded like a recalcitrant child.

Morgan turned to find that Jason had slumped down into a chair. "*Can't,* is more like it. Honestly, Jason. Why didn't you call and tell me you were sick and needed help."

Jason's eyes were closed, but he shook his head stubbornly in answer to her question.

Morgan found the spare sheets without too much trouble and changed the bed. When next she looked around, Jason was shivering. "Where are your pajamas? You need something on besides that bathrobe."

"I-I'm fine," he said and attempted to get up out of the chair.

"Don't you dare move until I find you some clothes to put on, Jason Falco."

He muttered something, which Morgan couldn't hear, but subsided. Delving through his drawers, she found a pair of warm socks. As for pajamas, though, she could only find silk ones. "Jason, don't you have any flannel pajamas?"

"I haven't worn flannel pajamas since I was twelve years old," he declared in a loftily offended voice.

Morgan's continued probing paid off. Pushed off in a corner, under a stack of sweaters, was a gift box that contained what she was looking for, given to him no doubt by some loving aunt. Helping him up, she soothed. "I know you're a big boy, now, but these will keep you warm." Leading him over to the bed, she sat him down and took off his robe. "Here," she slipped an undershirt over his head, "let's put this on first."

"I think I can manage to dress myself," he grumbled."

"Then let me see you do it."

In the end, it was mostly Morgan who managed to get him dressed and under the covers. "God, Jason, you're burning up! How long have you had this fever?"

"I don't know." His words slurred as he huddled under the covers. "I'm so *cold.*"

Morgan went into the bathroom and sorted through his medicine cabinet. She found aspirin, but no thermometer or cold tablets. Going through the linen cupboard one more time, she found a heating pad and a box of tissues.

Taking her finds back into the bedroom, she plugged the heating pad in and lifted Jason's covers. "Jason raise your feet, so I can put this under them."

"If it's dynamite, you're putting it at the wrong end. I need it under my head to open it up."

"It's nothing that lethal. Just a heating pad. It will help keep your feet warm."

"Why don't you get under the covers with me," he taunted weakly. "I understand body heat is the best thing a person can use to keep another person warm."

She refused to rise to his bait. "In this case, I think I can do more good for you with both feet firmly on the floor."

"T-that's certainly a switch in thinking."

"Hush, now, you shouldn't be talking so much. Just nod, yes or no. Do you feel like eating any soup?"

At his negative response, she continued. "How about something to drink?" At another shake of his head, Morgan frowned. "Well, you're going to have to drink something, because you're probably dehydrated. In a minute, I'll go make some hot tea. Right now I want you to use this box of tissues instead of that pillowcase."

"It works better than the tissues," he asserted childishly. "I don't have to be constantly reaching for a new one. I can keep it with me. Besides it's soft and my nose hurts."

"It's also not very sanitary, I'm afraid. Let's compromise. I'll go get you a clean pillowcase." He didn't say anything. "Jason, do you have a vaporizer anywhere?"

"Vaporizers are for babies."

"Oh, right." Morgan smiled wryly. "For some reason, I keep forgetting how grown up you are right now." She went into the kitchen to make him a cup of tea and returned. "Now," she sat down beside him, "I want you to drink some of this. It's good and hot and will warm you."

"I think I'd rather you warm me," he said, making a face after he had taken a drink.

"Sorry, but that's not one of your choices at the moment."

Jason lay back down and peered suspiciously at her over the pillowcase he was holding against his nose. "This must be some clever ploy on your part. Have you changed your *modus operandi*?"

"I'm doing this because I care very deeply for you, Jason, and I can't stand to see you feel this bad." She ran her fingers through his hair, tenderly combing it off his face. "One of these days maybe you'll understand that. Now, I think I'm going to run down to the nearest drugstore and buy you a vaporizer and some chest rub."

"I knew you wouldn't be able to keep your hands off me." Jason's words were slurring again and his eyes had shut. "But there's no reason to go, because I don't need any of those things."

Morgan looked at him worriedly. She hated to leave him alone. There was no telling how high his fever might climb, and his breathing was alarmingly shallow. She started to get up, but his hand come out and closed around her forearm. "Don't go."

Slurred though his words had been, she had still been able to understand them. "I'm not going to leave you." She layed her hand on his reassuringly. "I was just going in the next room to call Jerome and give him a list of stuff to bring over. I'm also going to call a doctor. Do you have one you prefer?"

"I don't want a doctor."

"Jason, you're sick, and you need something to knock down that fever."

"I hate shots."

Morgan smiled and leaned down to place a kiss on his forehead, feeling the dry heat of his skin against her lips. "I just know that you can be a big brave boy. I'll even hold your hand."

He opened his eyes. "I'm *not* getting a shot."

"Okay, okay. I'll make a deal with you. Let me call a doctor, and I'll make sure you get only pills."

"They can't be *too* big. My throat's sore."

"Not too big," she promised, amused at finding out that the sophisticated, commanding man she loved was like a frightened little boy when it came to doctors and being sick.

A couple of hours later, Morgan lay back in the bedside chair watching Jason. Both Jerome and the doctor had already come and gone. Jason seemed to be resting comfortably now, with the vaporizer steaming away by his bed, but the doctor had told her that he would continue to feel rotten for the next twenty-four to forty-eight hours.

"Morgan!"

She instantly sat upright, then leaned toward him. "What is it?"

"I just wanted to know if you're still here."

"I'm here and I'm staying until you're better."

And she did. There were times during the next day or two when Morgan let herself believe that Jason's sickness was bringing them closer. He seemed to want her constantly by his side, and if he woke and she wasn't there, he would call out for her.

Yet, as he got better and his body temperature became normal, his attitude toward her grew distinctly cooler, until finally, when Morgan could no longer think of an excuse to stay, she had to leave with only a very polite "Thank you for all you've done" to go home with.

Seven

All the next week Morgan tried to maintain an optimistic viewpoint, telling herself that she would hear from Jason at any time. It was impossible, to her way of thinking, that he wasn't yearning for her, just as she was for him. However, as time passed, there was not so much as a word from him. It was time for new action.

One morning she picked up the phone and placed a call to a local florist. "Paul's Florist," the pleasant voice of a young man greeted her. "Paul speaking."

"Good morning," she answered, "This is Morgan Saunders. I was wondering what the possibility would be of sending some tropical plants and flowers to someone here in St. Paul?"

"Tropical? What did you have in mind?"

"I don't know exactly. How about anthurium, or orchids . . . or maybe some pots of ferns."

"The pots of ferns I could handle, the others I would have to see about getting on special order, but there'd be no guarantees."

"I see." Morgan pondered for a moment, then decided. "In that case, let's start off with the ferns. I'd like three pots delivered every day to Mr. Jason Falco. His office is on the top floor of the DeWitt Building. Whenever you're able to get hold of any, add a tropical plant or two to the day's order, and if you can, mix up the sizes and the types of the ferns."

"Okay. Do you want a message sent with them?"

"Definitely. I'd like a card put on each plant, and I want the cards to say three words: '*Don't ever forget!*'"

"That's all? Just, 'Don't ever forget!'? You don't want your name or anything else on the cards?"

"No. I think that will be enough."

"Okay, Miss Saunders. How long do you want this order to run?"

"Until I tell you to stop."

Morgan sat in the full light of the afternoon sun, working on the embroidery. She had to chuckle. If the last few days at the warehouse had seemed particularly hectic, she could only imagine what it was like at Jason's office.

The door to her apartment had been left open, and she could hear Sami huffing and puffing, struggling down the hall from her workshop.

"Here it is." Sami staggered in carrying a huge papier-mache heart, which she had constructed and lacquered an eye-catching color of red. "It's finally dry and ready to be loaded up."

"Great. Set it down. You've got your choice. You can either help me embroider these men's bikini briefs or you can fill the heart with the chocolate kisses I've bought. I figure it'll take, at the very least, a thousand."

Sami made an instant decision. "I'll do the chocolate kisses. No telling what kind of word would come out if I tried doing those stitches."

"What's going on here?" Jerome had just walked in. "I came up to tell you that I've closed the shop, but I can see I should have done it much earlier. What are you two up to?"

"How are you at embroidering?" Morgan asked.

"Lousy, I would imagine. Embroidering what?"

Sami answered him. "Morgan's sewing a different day of the week on each of these seven bikini briefs"—she held up a bright emerald silk pair—"and she's going to send them to Jason. Isn't that a great idea?"

"Do I have to answer that question?"

"Oh, Jerome," Sami moaned sorrowfully. "You're *so* conservative!"

"And that monstrous red heart?"

"Sami is going to fill it with chocolate kisses"—Morgan rejoined the conversation—"and I'll write a note that reads, 'To remind you of our kisses that were sweeter than these.' "

Jerome sat down, took off his glasses and rubbed his hand across his eyes. "My pre-law major may come in real handy, Morgan, when Jason decides to prosecute you for harassment."

"She's not harassing him!" Sami flared indignantly. "She's not doing anything that men down through the ages haven't done to women they were pursuing. You know how men are always sending us flowers and candy and sometimes even lingerie. Jason has probably done it a hundred times himself. Well, Morgan's just turning the tables on him, that's all."

Morgan spoke up. "I've arranged for him to receive masses of ferns, plus other tropical plants. Also, I thought it would be a nice touch to send him little gifts. Today, for instance, he's receiving an enormous box. But when he opens it, he'll find a series of boxes, each one smaller and individually wrapped—"

Sami interrupted her. "We did that yesterday and used lots of different colored papers and bows."

"—until he gets to a tiny box that's filled with black sand collected from a Martinique beach where we picnicked one day. The note will read, 'Remember?' "

"Tell him about the singing telegrams," Sami urged.

"Maybe I should have the name of a good lawyer ready," Jerome mused to the room at large.

"The closer you get to becoming a lawyer, Jerome, the more respectable you're getting," Sami chided. "Where's your sense of fun?"

"Maybe even a bail bondsman," Jerome added to no one in particular.

"I don't see how the singing telegrams can fail," Sami declared confidently. "Think how much a woman would love to be serenaded, and all arranged by the man she loves."

Jerome didn't appear convinced. "What kind of songs are you having him bombarded with?"

"*Serenaded*," Sami corrected him with a frown. "The word is serenaded."

Morgan laughed. "Love songs, of course. Yesterday, the song that I requested was the one that goes, 'You were meant for me, I was meant for you.' You know the one. This morning's song was 'Love Is A Many Splendored Thing.' "

"Why don't you just hit him over the head with a sledge hammer and be done with it?" Jerome inquired.

"Tomorrow, the song will be 'Always,' and the day after tomorrow, 'Some Enchanted Evening.' "

"I know that one." Jerome grinned. "It goes, 'Some enchanted evening, you will meet a stranger, across a crowded airplane.' "

Sami glared at him. "I can see you're not taking this seriously, but Morgan's whole future is at stake here. She loves Jason, Jason loves her; he just needs a little gentle prodding, that's all."

"If you call this 'gentle prodding,' I'd hate to see your maximum effort, but, okay. I know when I'm overruled. What can I do to help?"

"You can go over to Sami's apartment and select one of her birds—try to pick the one with the sweetest expression on his face—and bring it here." Morgan glanced at Sami. "If that's all right with you, that is."

"Of course. My birds are always willing to do good deeds. But what are you going to do with him?"

"I'm going to put him into a cage and send it to Jason with a note that reads, 'Without your love,

I'm as caged as this little guy here. Please set me free.' "

"I love it!" Sami clapped her hands excitedly. "I just love it!"

"Somehow I knew you would," Jerome said dryly, already on his way out the door.

Several days later, Morgan's phone rang. "Hello?"

"Morgan, you've *got* to stop this."

"Jason! How nice to hear from you. How are you?"

"Terrible. Do you have any idea how embarrassing it is to be on the receiving end of all these 'gifts' you keep sending me?"

She gave him an impish grin through the telephone. "I thought you'd enjoy them."

"These ferns—"

"I've always felt that a person can't have too many ferns, don't you agree?"

"Morgan, enough is enough." In spite of his stern words, Jason sounded as if he were very close to breaking into a laugh. "But, I'll give you an 'A' for originality and cleverness."

"How about for persistence?"

"*Especially* for persistence—but it's all got to stop. You're disrupting my office. My employees can hardly get any work done, what with their damned twittering about the things that are constantly arriving and their speculation about what you're going to do next." There was a significant pause. "What *are* you going to do next?"

"Well, uh—"

"And those *sappy* love songs! Come on. Give me a break."

"I'll have you know those are *old standards*."

"Maybe. But can you imagine how I feel when, at ten o'clock every morning, all my employees start gathering outside my office to hear the latest warblings by that tenor you hired?"

"Pleased?" Morgan guessed.

"Damned uncomfortable!"

"Gosh, I'm sorry. I auditioned him myself. I thought he was very good, but perhaps you'd prefer a baritone."

"Morgan . . ." Jason's voice trailed off in an exasperated chuckle. "I don't know how you do it, but you always manage to get around me."

Morgan laughed with him. "You'll like the song for tomorrow. It's entitled 'Till.' Do you remember how it goes? 'Till the moon deserts the sky, till all the seas run dry, till then I'll worship you. Till, the tropic sun grows cold—' "

He spoke quietly. "That's enough, Morgan."

"And the song for the next day is my favorite. It's called 'Only You,' and it sums up perfectly how I feel about you. The lyrics start out, 'Only you can make this world seem right, only you can make the darkness bright, only you and you alone can thrill me like you do . . .'" She hesitated for a moment. "It seems to me as if I've said it so many times, in so many ways—I was just trying to show you in a different way this time."

"Morgan." His voice had hardened again. "I want all of this nonsense stopped immediately! Do you understand?"

"All right. If you insist, Jason."

• • •

Morgan stared unseeingly at the river before her. Jason . . . Jason, Jason, Jason. His name ran in an unending circle in her mind. There'd been no word from him since she had stopped sending him the gifts and plants—not even so much as a thank-you note. What was she going to do now? She was fresh out of ideas, yet she had an overwhelming need to see him.

Reaching impulsively for the phone, she picked it up and punched out the number of his office. His secretary answered, "Mr. Falco's office."

Gazing out the window at the Mississippi and thinking of how filled with ferns Jason's office must be by now, Morgan affected her best southern drawl. "Hello. This is Ms. Fern Rivers. I'm an old friend of Mr. Falco's; but then I'm sure that Jay has probably mentioned me to you."

"I'm afraid not," the secretary apologized, "or at least, not that I can remember."

"No? Oh well, even if he hasn't, you sound as if you're a highly intelligent young woman. I'm positive you'll be able to help me." Morgan's voice was dripping with so much sugar, she was sure that her teeth would acquire several cavities before she hung up. "I don't want to bother *dear* Jay with this itsy-bitsy problem."

"I'll try my best, Ms. Rivers," the earnest secretary assured Morgan, completely won over.

"Good. I just knew you would. You see, the strangest thing has happened. The last time I talked with Jay, we set up a luncheon appointment for this week, but silly ol' me, I just can't seem to remember which day it is."

"That will be very easy to check. Just let me get his appointment book." There was a pause. "I'm sorry, Ms. Rivers, but I can't seem to find your name anywhere."

"You simply *must* be mistaken, honey." Morgan allowed a mere hint of accusation to trickle into her voice. "You do write down all of his appointments, don't you?"

"Yes, of course I do, but even though he has several luncheon appointments this week, I don't see one set up with you."

"Look again," Morgan urged.

"Let's see," the secretary started to think aloud, just as Morgan had hoped she would. "Tomorrow at one, he will be lunching with a group of bankers."

Morgan seized the tidbit of information, like a dog with a bone. "Oh, yes." she drawled airily. "He told me all about that. That's at the Roco Room, isn't it?"

"No, they'll be meeting at Tres Elan."

"Sure 'nuf? Well, my, my, my. I guess I just must have gotten all mixed up. I can't tell you how stupid I feel."—At least that much was the truth, Morgan reflected wryly.—"I tell you what, honey. Let's just keep this between us girls, and I'll get back to him the first of next week. Okay?"

"That will be fine, Ms. Rivers."

"You're very understanding," Morgan practically sang into the phone and made a mental note to tell Jason to give his secretary a raise. "Goodbye."

• • •

Morgan arrived at Tres Elan the next day with no other thought on her mind than to see Jason. Shedding her coat in the foyer, she made her way toward the maître d', giving him her name. "Saunders."

"Yes, Miss Saunders. That was a reservation for one?"

Morgan nodded, already at the door, her eyes scanning the room. She was in luck. Jason was already there, sitting with a group of men at a table situated to one side of the room. There was a small, vacant, horseshoe-shaped booth directly across from him and Morgan slipped a bill into the maître d's hand. "That booth please."

"Certainly, Ms. Saunders."

Morgan followed her waiter, careful to keep her eyes ahead of her. Sliding into the booth so that she faced toward the man she had come to see, she blinked a quick glimpse in the direction of his table and saw that Jason had spotted her.

She smiled dazzlingly at her hovering waiter. "I'll just have a salad and a glass of wine to start with, thank you."

Morgan proceeded to take off the jacket that went with her burgundy-colored wool suit, stretching this way and that—perhaps, she admitted honestly to herself, a little more than was strictly necessary. But she knew that the mauve silk blouse covered the contours of her curves very attractively, and she wanted to make sure that Jason knew it, too.

Twisting around to throw it along the back of

the booth, she decided that perhaps it was a good thing she hadn't worn a bra today, even though it had been a subliminal decision, one that had been made below her threshhold of consciousness. It was just that loving Jason had brought her innate sensuality to the surface, and now it seemed as though she acted instinctively where he was concerned.

Morgan raised her eyes to meet Jason's stare. There could be no doubt in his mind that she was here for any other reason than to see him. Her eyes engulfed him. Although he seemed to be recovered from his illness, she couldn't help but note the recent thinness in his face and the new lines around his mouth.

His mouth. It tightened, as Jason turned back to his conversation. For want of something to do, Morgan picked up a bread stick and began to absently nibble the salt off it, idly looking around the fashionable decor of the restaurant. Her booth had walls that raised to shield her on two sides, but her view of Jason was uninterrupted, as was his of her.

Morgan had her tongue flat against the side of the bread stick, when she happened to look back at Jason. His eyes were fixed on her and he had gone rather gray in color.

Tossing the breadstick down with a shrug, Morgan turned to the waiter who had arrived with her wine and salad and gave him an enthusiastic greeting. Now she would have something to do while she watched Jason.

About to take a sip of her wine, Morgan had the glass up to her lips, when Jason threw her a look of such annoyance that she became disconcerted and spilled the wine onto her blouse.

Oh, no! Morgan muttered, "Here I am—I haven't seen Jason in ages, I'm trying to act coolly sophisticated to make a good impression, and now I have this awful stain on my blouse. And to top it off, I'm talking to myself!"

Taking her napkin and dipping one corner of it in her water glass, Morgan began dabbing at her blouse. The wine had managed to drip on top of one of her breasts, and she rubbed furiously at the whole area, determined to get it out.

Taking a quick survey of the room, Morgan realized with relief that everyone who could see her was engrossed in their own conversations. When she glanced at Jason, however, she saw that he was watching her with an open mouth and that his glass of water was suspended in midair. Morgan looked down to see what had attracted his attention. Damn! One half of her blouse was plastered transparently against her, with both nipples jutting enticingly against the fabric. *She was mortified!*

"I'll never be able to get the stain out and at the same time save my modesty," Morgan mumbled despairingly. She reached for her jacket. "Double damn!" She had forgotten that the top button on this blouse needed to be sewn on more securely. All that stretching she had done when she first arrived hadn't helped the matter, and, now, wouldn't you just know it, the button had popped off. Consequently, a good two inches of her cleavage was exposed—two inches more than should have been.

Morgan looked quickly at Jason and saw that he had given up all pretense of eating, and if the men he was with noticed that he seemed to be preoccupied with something across the room, they were well-mannered enough to give no sign.

She slipped on her jacket, and her waiter appeared minutes later. "Would you care to order now?"

"No thank you," Morgan shook her head ruefully. "I think I'm quite through." Picking up her purse, she slid out of the booth. If she had had any aspirations of driving Jason mad with her cool, remote beauty—cool, remote beauty, much in the vein of Melinda Johnson—they had dissolved, all within the space of about ten minutes.

Nevertheless, she attempted to salvage some remaining vestige of her pride. "That handsome gentleman with the extremely pale complexion"— she pointed out Jason—"has kindly offered to pay for my lunch. Just add it to his tab." And with a smile to all concerned, Morgan left.

She managed to wait until she reached her apartment before completely falling apart. But once there, Morgan started to cry. She felt drained. Continually expending all her emotions toward Jason, she was getting nothing in return from him. This pursuit was taking more and more out of her, and she didn't know how much longer she could go on. Still, she had to believe that what she was trying to do was best for all concerned. She *had* to.

Morgan cried herself to sleep, and when she woke, she felt one hundred percent better. Her optimism and her sense of humor had returned, and she found herself giggling aloud to her empty bedroom. After all, if she had *planned* what had happened at the restaurant, it probably wouldn't have turned out half as well—and she *had* managed to capture Jason's complete attention.

Eight

One early afternoon over a week later, Morgan's spirits were again at a low ebb. She was sitting in her shop, sifting listlessly through the mail. Despite her determination, it was getting harder and harder to fight the inevitable discouragement which seemed to be growing progressively worse in the face of Jason's continued resistance to her.

Spying one particularly fat-looking envelope, Morgan opened it. It was a final bill from Paul's Florist.

"That's all I need," Morgan muttered and pushed all the mail off her desk in a fit of dejection. Then, pulling a handful of paper clips out of a desk drawer, she began stringing them together, and by the time Jerome burst cheerfully in from school a little while later, she had quite a long chain strung across the desk.

"Hard at work, I see."

"Listen, Junior," Morgan snapped in a rare display of bad humor, "if you don't have anything more intelligent to say than that, you can just turn around and go back out the way you came."

"Wow! 'Operation Jason' must really be going bad. I think—"

Before Jerome had a chance to finish what he had been about to say and Morgan had an opportunity to reply, their eyes were drawn to the door. Sami, weaving hazily into the office area of the shop, wore only a sleep-fogged look and a flower-strewn sheet that was wrapped haphazardly around her.

"Just getting up?" Jerome teased her lightly. "You really ought to try mornings sometime—after all, they *are* the other half of the day."

"Gee. Did you learn that in school today?"

Morgan's sarcastic jibe didn't bother Jerome. "And by the way, Sami. I've always maintained that no one wears a sheet quite like you do, but, just out of curiosity, where is the nightgown I gave you for Christmas?"

"Oh, for heaven sakes! Don't just stand there asking a lot of stupid questions," Morgan exploded. "Get her some coffee!"

"Coffee," Sami mumbled and fell into a nearby chair.

"Hey! I know as well as you do that Sami has trouble sleeping at night. I was only kidding. She knows that I didn't mean anything by it."

Morgan jumped up, irrationally irritated. "I can't believe the future of our nation's judicial system is in the hands of your generation! The complete arrogance of the young staggers me."

"Coffee?" Sami interjected faintly.

"I'm not that much younger than you are," Jerome pointed out. "Anyway, I think there's something you've lost sight of here. My name is *not* Jason Falco. I'm on your side, remember?"

Sinking back down in her chair, Morgan ran her hands distractedly through her hair. "I'm sorry, Jerome. I really am. I didn't mean to take it out on you. It's just that I'm getting exactly nowhere with Jason and I don't know what to do next. And to top it all off"—she pointed toward the floor—"I just got an astronomical bill from the florist. It's a good thing the shop is doing so well."

"Coffee?" Sami pleaded quaveringly.

"I don't understand it." Jerome shook his head. "Any man that could take the things that you've done to him and still hold out, can't be human."

"Oh, he's human all right . . . or at least he was in Martinique."

Jerome laughed. "Have you considered the possibility that he picked up some rare tropical disease while he was down there that affected his brain, not to mention his libido?"

"I wish I could believe that," Morgan grumbled. "It would make this problem a whole lot easier to understand."

"You know, something Sami said keeps coming back to me. She commented that there had to be something more to this whole situation than we knew, and I'm beginning to agree."

"Maybe. But how am I ever going to find out if I can't even get Jason to talk to me?"

A silence fell over the office until Morgan happened to glance over at Sami. She looked comatose. "Would you like a cup of coffee?"

There was no answer.

Morgan poured some coffee and handed it to Sami, then returned to her desk and paper clip chain.

"What's this?" Jerome had been gathering up the mail from the floor. "It looks like some sort of invitation."

Looking at the envelope, Morgan shrugged disinterestedly. "It is. It's for the annual bash that the Small Businessmen's Association throws. I probably won't go this year."

"Why not?"

"I'm not exactly in a partying mood," she pointed out gloomily. "Besides, I get tired of fighting off Dirk Concannon. The minute I walk in the door, he attaches himself to me and I can't get rid of him. That man has more hands than an octopus."

"Have you tried taking a date?"

"Sure. Nothing fazes Dirk—three gin and tonics and he thinks he's Rudolph Valentino."

"Ask Jason to take you."

Jerome and Morgan looked at each other.

Sami repeated herself. "Ask Jason to take you. If he's your date, two things can happen and they're both good. One: Dirk will be so intimidated by Jason that he will leave you alone, or Two: Dirk won't leave you alone, and Jason will be eaten up with jealousy."

"She's awake," Jerome said to Morgan.

"There's no way on God's green earth that I could get Jason to agree to escort me to that party."

Sami hitched the sheet up under her arms, took another swig of coffee and directed the full force of her intelligent golden eyes on Morgan. "You can get him to take you."

Morgan stood on the sidewalk looking up at the DeWitt Building. She had already walked around the block once, trying to get her nerve up, and city blocks being as long as they were, she didn't want to do it again. "Oh, well. Faint heart never won fair gentleman," she misquoted to herself and plunged into the building.

Once on Jason's floor, she breezed past various receptionists and ultimately his secretary with the air of someone who knew exactly what she was doing, unable to miss, as she did so, the overabundance of ferns that dotted every available nook and cranny. Flinging open his door, Morgan walked in and quickly closed it behind her before he could order her out.

"Good morning, Jason."

Her heart nearly stopped at the sight of him. He had been studying some papers at his desk, but had looked up at her entrance. The depth of her love for him assailed her, and she could have cried at his stubbornness which was allowing precious time to pass that otherwise could have been used to the great joy of them both.

Jason threw down the pen he had been using and leaned back in the padded luxury of his executive chair. "You must be very thickheaded, Morgan. I thought I had made myself perfectly clear about not wanting to see you again."

"Funny, I was just thinking the same thing about you." She took her coat off, letting it drop onto a chair, and sat down on the corner of his desk, at the same time hitching up her straight skirt, so that a goodly expanse of shapely thigh showed. "The thickheaded part, that is. At any rate, I didn't come here to trade insults with you."

"That's good, because you'd lose the exchange. I can think of an infinite number of names to call you. My vocabulary happens to be endless where you're concerned."

Morgan noticed that, as hard as his words were, Jason couldn't seem to keep his eyes from roaming restlessly over the softness of her powder blue sweater and the curves that it covered.

"Why Jason! How sweet . . . although I seem to remember your saying something slightly different in the rain forest."

"I'm in no mood for another one of your little performances, so make it brief. Why are you here?"

The chill in his words was enough to make Morgan want to turn tail and run. But she didn't. "Actually, I need a favor. I've received an invitation to the annual banquet and dance for the Small Businessmen's Association"—Morgan twisted her fingers together, the only sign of how nervous she was—"and I need an escort."

"It shouldn't prove too difficult for you to find someone to take you. With your charm and beauty, it'll be no problem." The words cut through the air with mortal sharpness.

"T-thank you for the compliment, but you see, this is sort of last minute. It's in less than a week, and there just isn't time. Since David's out of town, I naturally thought of you."

"I see nothing natural about it," he rapped out. "What gives you the effrontery to think that I would agree to take you, Morgan? You've really got nerves of steel."

Clasping her hands tightly together to keep them from trembling, she braved her reply. "I didn't think you'd mind, once you realized how important it was to me. The party would be strictly business, of course, and, besides . . . I knew you would do just about anything to keep me from finding David and asking him to take me." Morgan swallowed hard. She hated having to bring David into this.

The menacing intent in his tone was palpable as he drawled, "That sounds suspiciously like a threat, Morgan, and I would strongly advise against doing anything as foolish as trying to threaten me."

"You do realize that I could find David, don't you? All I'd have to do is hire a private investigator, and I'm sure that within a matter of days I would know exactly where he is."

"It'll never happen. I told you. David is someplace where you can't get your seductive little claws into him. So you can drop that gambit right now."

Morgan rose from her provocative perch on the side of his desk and made her way around it until she was beside him. "What's the matter, Jason? I do believe that the big, brave man is afraid of one, itty, bitty, little girl. You must be worried that I'll sink my claws into *you*."

"No!" He shot up from his seat and was across

the room so fast, Morgan wouldn't have been surprised to find that a lightning bolt had struck where he had been sitting.

"Come on, Jason, admit it." She strolled to within a few feet of him and folded her arms across her chest in an attitude of supreme assurance, doing her best to ignore her quaking legs. "It's not so much that you're afraid that I'll sink my claws into David, as it is that you're worried about yourself. I would imagine that it'll be a long time before the scars, which I put on your back in the throes of our passion, will disappear. I've *already* made my mark on you, and it's something you can't forget, no matter how hard you try. Tell the truth. You're still every bit as affected by me as I am by you."

"Get this straight, Morgan. The minute I found out that you had deceived me, I lost whatever warm feelings I might have had for you."

Morgan moved closer to him, enveloping him with her fragrance, and actually managed a little laugh. "I don't believe you, Jason, and I *dare* you to prove what you just said. Go with me to this party, and if at the end of the evening you can still say you feel nothing for me, it will be the last you'll ever hear from me. I promise."

"Your promises mean absolutely zero to me. Nothing you try is going to work, Morgan, so you might as well save yourself a lot of grief and embarrassment. But don't be too upset. There are bound to be a lot of men who'll succumb to the fatality of your practiced feminine wiles."

"You have no idea what you're talking about, Jason, and frankly neither do I."

"Let me put it this way"—the corners of his mouth lifted sardonically—"second-hand goods have never interested me very much."

Morgan was stunned. "That's not fair, Jason! I haven't done anything to deserve that."

"Haven't you?"

"*Absolutely not.* I told you about Clinton Monroe in the gentleness and sweetness of our first moments together. If you'll take a moment to look back and to remember how you first felt about me, maybe you'll come to understand how wrong you are, or at the very least begin to have a few doubts." Jason didn't answer her.

Moving restively over to the window, Morgan looked down on the busy street in front of his building.

She had a terrible feeling that her chances of winning Jason back were dwindling rapidly. With every tick of the clock, she ran the risk of him forgetting more and more of their holiday together— of him placing another layer of stone over his heart in his defense against her—until the time would come when he would be completely immune to her.

And there was something else, too. Every time she inflamed his senses, bringing him to the point of fevered passion, she also brought herself to the same heated level of sexual excitement. She was doing it to *both* of them. Morgan didn't know about Jason, but she really wasn't sure how much more of it she could take. He might seek solace with another woman, but Morgan knew she would never again turn to another man in desire.

She had to try one more time. There must be a

way. . . . Gazing at a series of billboards that sat directly across from his office, Morgan was struck suddenly by what she considered to be an inspired idea. She turned back to see that Jason was once more sitting behind his desk. Retreated, had he?

She thrust her hands in the pockets of her skirt and strolled casually toward him, noticing as she did how Jason's eyes were drawn to the taut charcoal-colored cloth that stretched across the flat of her stomach.

"I just happened to notice that there's an empty billboard across the street that some company is advertising for rent."

"So?"

"So . . . if you don't take me to that party, I am going to rent that space and inform everyone that Jason Falco is not only afraid to be alone with Morgan Saunders, but that he's a coward and a fool not to admit that he loves her."

"Nice bluff, Morgan, but you won't do it," Jason smirked confidently. "You see, it would not only embarrass me, but it would embarrass you as well, and I don't think even you are willing to go quite that far. Now," he reached for his pen and pulled some papers toward him, "if you're quite through, I would like for you to leave."

Morgan picked up her coat and strolled toward the door. When she reached it, however, she turned back to him with a smile. "It's a shame you didn't get to know me better while we were in Martinique, Jason. Goodbye for now. I'll see you in a few days."

• • •

Morgan could never remember being this nervous before. It was three days later, and she was in her shop, making an effort to do business as usual. She had a sinking feeling that it was no use though, because she had already rung up three sales wrong this morning. Twice she had overpriced a wicker item, and once she had practically given away a very expensive mirror bordered with an elaborate montage of seashells.

She couldn't keep her mind on her work. The billboard should be up by now. Had Jason seen it yet? What if he never looked out his window? "Calm down," she counseled herself. "Even if he doesn't look out the window, he'll be able to see it as he drives to work.

"Oh, no! What if he's out-of-town?" Morgan glanced toward the phone. Maybe she should give his secretary a call and find out. The woman was always a veritable fount of information.

Looking at her watch, Morgan saw that it was nine-fifteen. The man to whom she had spoken had said his men would start putting up the sign about seven. "I'll give Jason thirty more minutes," she decided.

The door bell tinkled, indicating that someone had just entered. Putting on her most professional smile, she turned. "Can I help you?"

"Yes!" Jason bellowed, as he switched the "Open" sign in the window to "Closed" and locked the door. "You can have that damned billboard taken down at once."

Morgan eyed him warily. Even through his obvious anger, she could detect a certain *hunted* quality about him. Hopefully, that was a good sign.

"I told you I'd have it put up, Jason. You should have believed me—and not only about having that ad put up. I always tell the truth."

"Morgan"—he advanced menacingly toward her and put his hands around her throat, squeezing slightly—"I could kill you now and there's not a jury in the country that would convict me."

"You won't do it," she gasped softly, "because you love me. A person can't destroy someone he loves."

She felt his fingers tighten for a fraction of a second before he pushed her away. "You're right. I won't do it, but not for the reason you said. I need you alive to get on the phone and get that sign taken down."

"Sure," she agreed, rubbing her throat, "I'll be glad to . . . for a price. All you have to do is take me to that party."

He looked at her with eyes that resembled black marble. "Lord, Morgan, you really are a bitch!"

"Will you do it?"

"I guess I have to, if I don't want to be the laughing stock of the city. *But*"—he flashed a cruel smile—"you're going to have to remember your part of the bargain and live up to it."

"My part?"

"You said that if I spent the evening with you and still felt nothing for you by the end of the night, you'd leave me alone."

Despite the sadness that threatened to choke her, Morgan lifted her chin. "That's what I said and I won't go back on my word."

"That remains to be seen," Jason said heavily. "What time do I have to pick you up?"

"The party starts at eight. If you pick me up at seven forty-five, that should give us plenty of time."

He started out the door, but turned back. "That billboard had better be down within the hour or our deal is off."

Morgan smiled sweetly. "Why of course, Jason."

Morgan looked at herself one more time in the mirror, just to make certain. No, the dress only *seemed* diaphanous, but it wasn't. Rather it was the way the dress flowed liquidly around her that gave the impression that it could be seen through.

The dress was blue chiffon laid over green silk and sliding over her body it resembled the moving waters of the Carribean. Slightly above the knee in length, the frock had a low, strapless bodice; and Morgan, critically viewing herself, experimented with drawing deep breaths. Perfect! Although the dress had a daring neckline, she would be quite safe.

Having been ready for what seemed like hours, Morgan picked up her coat and purse and paced into the living room to wait. She calculated that Jason should be arriving at any moment.

A loud knock on the door brought her pre-date jitters to an end. Deliberately dawdling, she stalled as long as she dared before answering the door. Then, adopting her best flustered and harried look, she hurried to the door and opened it . . . but only far enough to allow her to stick her head around it. "Jason! Are you early?"

He looked at his watch, elegantly handsome in

his dark evening wear despite the scowl that marred his face. "I'm right on time."

"But I'm not ready!" she wailed. "I've got at least a hundred things to do yet."

"Morgan," Jason growled warningly. "I'm escorting you to this party only under protest. Therefore, I'm in no mood to stand around waiting while you mess with your hair, or powder your nose, or whatever it is that women usually do to keep men waiting for hours at a time. You look fine, so just get your coat and let's go. I want this evening over with as soon as possible."

"Are you sure we can't spare just five minutes so that I can—"

"Morgan!"

She meekly complied. "Whatever you say, Jason."

Morgan waited until they were about halfway across town before she began to act fidgety. It was nothing too obvious at first, just a few adjustments to the way she was sitting, but it was enough to pull Jason out of his brooding silence. She could tell by the way he tensed that she had drawn his attention back to her.

Waiting until she could tell that he had once again started to retreat behind his abstracted thoughts, Morgan began to squirm uncomfortably. Jason didn't comment. He just threw her one of those annoyed looks that she was coming to know so well.

The closer they got to the hall where the party was being held, the antsier Morgan behaved, until Jason finally barked, "What in the hell is wrong with you tonight?"

Morgan gave a big sigh and did a creditable job

of looking injured. "Well, I *tried* to tell you, Jason. It's your fault, after all, for making me rush like you did."

"What are you talking about?"

She explained in a timid little girl's voice, "Well . . . I didn't exactly have time to finish dressing."

"Just what are you trying to say?" Jason glanced at her suspiciously. "You *do* have a dress on underneath that coat, don't you?"

"*Of course*, I do. Goodness, Jason! Do you honestly think I'd go out without a dress on?"

"What's the problem, then?" His patience was wearing noticeably thin.

"Actually, it's nothing really very serious. It's just that you insisted we leave in such a hurry, I think I forgot to put on any underwear. You know how it is. You can't wear just *anything* under your clothes these days, because the lines might show through. Anyway, I was trying on different things, and, uh, I . . ."

Jason exploded. "You mean you don't have *anything* on under your dress?"

"I don't think so," she answered pleasantly. "No bra, no panties, not even a pair of hose," she went on to add, in case he had missed the full significance of the matter.

He hadn't. His hands tightened on the steering wheel and his jaw clenched violently. "We'll have to go back then."

"*No!* That is, we can't! Oh, please, Jason. Tonight is really important for me, and I'm afraid we're going to be late as it is. These people get extremely upset if everyone isn't there and in their proper place so that the banquet can start on time."

"I don't see anything else we can do."

Poor man—Morgan took a moment to sympathize silently with him—he actually sounded rather helpless. However, it was a very *brief* moment of sympathy, and she felt no guilt whatsoever as she hastened to reassure him. "No, really. It will be all right. You'll see. My legs are still so tanned from our holiday, that it will look as if I have hose on, and my dress is two layers thick. No one will even notice." . . . Except you, she murmured to herself, comfortably wiggling her bottom into the plushness of the car's seat.

Nine

The banquet had indeed started, but contrary to what Morgan had told Jason, there had been no reason to worry about arriving late. The Small Businessmen's Association contained a membership of relaxed and confident men and women, who always showed great tolerance and flexibility toward each other and life in general. Theirs was a group for mutual benefit, nothing more, nothing less.

In the foyer, Jason checked their coats after an eagle-eyed scrutiny of the dress that Morgan wore. Morgan wasn't worried. She knew he wouldn't get the full effect of the dress until she started to move.

A waiter showed them to their reserved places. And when Morgan saw where they would be sitting, she didn't know whether to laugh or to cry. Dirk

Concannon was sitting directly across the table from them.

"Morgan! Great to see you."

Dirk owned a small chain of exercise facilities and fancied himself something of a ladies' man, taking full advantage of the scantily clad women that surrounded him day in and day out. Morgan had gone to his spa once and, after Dirk had managed to corner her in the sauna, had vowed never to go back. Nonetheless, they were on several of the same committees, and she had to be polite to him in public.

Feeling safe with Jason by her side, Morgan bestowed a warmer than usual smile on him and settled into her chair. "Dirk, I'd like you to meet my date for this evening, Jason Falco. Jason, this is Dirk Concannon—" Her mind went blank. How should she introduce him? In the end, she decided she could afford to be nice. "—a friend."

Dirk blinked at Morgan's introduction. Even though it was true they had known each other a long time, the word "friend" was stretching the point quite a bit and they both knew it.

Jason nodded curtly, but didn't bother to respond. He had seen Dirk's reaction to the seductive way in which Morgan's dress flowed over her body, and his face was becoming grimmer by the minute. Sensing this, Morgan decided that for once it looked as if things might finally go her way, and she couldn't have been happier about the situation.

All through dinner, Morgan enjoyed both men's complete attention, although she did nothing wrong, taking extreme care to impartially direct her conversation to both of them. Dirk was obviously flattered by her attention, and he began flirting with her. On the other hand, everytime she turned to Jason, she found his eyes riveted to the low neckline of her dress, where the tops of her round, creamy breasts gleamed alluringly.

Whenever she was sure that Dirk's attention was elsewhere, Morgan used Jason's single-minded concentration on her to incite him by bending forward to take a bite of her dinner, or by leaning toward him to speak a few words. From her practice sessions, Morgan knew exactly how far she could go in her movements wearing this very décolleté dress. She carried propriety to the very outer limits, toying dangerously with disaster, and, in the process, enjoyed herself immensely.

At one point, when Dirk was talking with the person sitting beside him, Morgan turned toward Jason, licking some of the vanilla ice cream dessert from around her mouth with her tongue. "Jason, this is a delicious dessert. Why aren't you eating any?"

"I'm not hungry," he snapped, watching with manifest fascination the way the fullness of her breasts moved everytime her arm did.

Morgan's tongue darted out, taking one last lick of the sweet concoction off her spoon before she put it down. "There'll be a few short speeches in a moment, but don't worry, they won't last long, and they're never dull. I think you'll enjoy them." Jason was sitting on her left, and she casually hooked her left arm over the back of her chair so that the top half of her body was twisted toward him. "Then there'll be dancing. They usually have a marvelous orchestra here."

Morgan absently ran a finger inside the top edge of her dress as she spoke—imitating to perfection the intimate gesture that Jason had used on her so many times—and had the satisfaction of seeing a few beads of sweat break out on his forehead. "I can't wait to get on the dance floor. It's been quite a while . . . well, let me think"—her forehead furrowed in concentration—"I guess the last time I danced was with you on the plantation terrace."

"Where's the bar?"

"Unless, of course, you want to count the time we danced at Paddy's and Company."

"Morgan, where's the bar?"

"The bar? They won't set it up until after everyone has finished eating and the speeches are over. Where was I? Ummmm . . . oh yes, I'm really looking forward to dancing with you again." Morgan leaned toward him and confided, "I thought we did it so well together."

"I won't be dancing tonight."

"Don't be a party pooper! Come on," she cajoled. "Just for old times' sake?"

The look Jason threw her would have shriveled any right-thinking person, but Morgan was well and truly into her act. "Gee. Oh well, maybe you'll change your mind later on."

Unfortunately for her, Dirk had finished with his conversation and had overheard the last part of theirs. "Hey, your problems are over. I'll be more than happy to dance with you!"

Morgan looked at Jason for help, hoping that

he would tell Dirk that he would be dancing with her, but only a mask of cold indifference met her eyes.

Morgan's shoulders drooped with discouragement as she watched the first speaker approach the podium. She had predicted correctly. The speeches finished quickly, and the party took on new life as the less formal part of the evening began.

Jason rose and politely held Morgan's chair for her. Standing up very fast, Morgan managed to lose her balance and fall against Jason's chest. Instinctively, his hands came out to catch her, and she let her full weight rest against him.

Looking up at him, she saw that his eyes had gone dark and that the golden flecks in them were casting out a burning light, covering her with an all-encompassing illumination that made her feel weak. Jason's gaze lowered over the smooth expanse of her throat to her half-bare heaving chest. His swiftly indrawn breath made Morgan look down. Evidently, the force of her fall against him had moved the material of the dress's bodice a fraction, allowing a tantalizing glimpse from above.

"I'm going to the bar," Jason grated hoarsely. "Are you coming?"

"I-in a minute."

"Fine." He pushed her away and the material of her dress slipped obediently back into place.

Watching Jason stride rapidly away, Morgan gnawed anxiously on her lower lip. Although everything appeared to be going well so far, she had to wonder if this plan was going to work. None of the others had, and she only had the next few hours to try and win Jason back. Morgan had promised him that tonight would be the end of it, and whether he believed her or not, she was a woman of her word.

She would have to be a fool, however, not to realize that her chances were getting slimmer by the minute. And she was no fool, even if, at times lately, she had been acting like one.

Something else was bothering her, too. A fact she had been deliberately pushing to the back of her mind. The first time she had gone after what she wanted it had ended in heartache, and she couldn't help but wonder if the same thing would happen this time.

Groups formed, broke up and formed again, and Morgan moved about the room with bright friendliness, meeting and talking with fellow business owners. Every once in a while, she would look over at Jason where he was lounging against the bar, and their eyes would lock. The passion that raced between them was a very real thing. It had substance and a life of its own. Jason could try to deny it all he wanted, but it was something that neither of them seemed to be able to help. It was just there—like the sun in the morning, the moon and stars on a cloudless night.

Morgan started toward him, but Dirk appeared at her side. "I'm here to claim my dance, pretty baby."

Morgan hated Dirk's habit of calling women by familiar pet names, and the forced smile she gave him almost cracked her face—although from a distance, it must have seemed genuine. "Some other time, perhaps. If you don't mind, Dirk, I'd rather not dance tonight." The *last* thing in the world she wanted to do was to dance with Dirk Concannon.

"But I've been waiting since dinner. You can't tell me *no* now!"

Dirk took the matter out of her hands by leading her onto the dance floor, and once there, holding her in what was no doubt his idea of a romantic embrace. In actuality, it was a bear hug, and Morgan found it terribly hard to breathe. But she couldn't complain. She had brought it all on herself and it served her right for bringing up the subject of dancing within his hearing. When was she ever going to learn?

Doing her utmost to keep in step with Dirk's erratic sense of rhythm and, at the same time, to relax against him, Morgan looked over his shoulder to see Jason watching them closely. Never one to miss a shot, Morgan adopted a sultry look and mouthed the words, *"You're beautiful,"* to him. To her great surprise, she saw a dark flush creep up his neck to his face, coloring it with an uncharacteristic blush. Immediately afterwards, though, he tossed down a glass of some potent-looking beverage and turned his back on her.

What now? Morgan considered. Unfortunately, she could only concentrate on one problem at a time, and for the moment, Dirk's wandering hands demanded her immediate attention. He was moving the blue chiffon over the green silk in a manner that Morgan found nauseating. She managed to wedge one of her hands between them, but he paid no attention.

"Oh, baby," he crooned into her ear, "you really

take my breath away. I've been after you for a long time, and I've finally got you in my arms."

"D-Dirk." Morgan pushed against him. "Why don't we go get something to drink?"

He pulled her closer. "Yeah, sure, baby, in a minute. Right now, I just want to feel you against me." His hands had moved down to her hips, roaming more and more freely.

Trying again, Morgan protested, pushing a little harder, "But I could really use a drink, Dirk. There are too many people on this dance floor. It's so close in here, and I'm getting hot!"

"That's the whole idea, baby. That's the whole idea."

Dear Lord in heaven, Morgan thought despairingly, Dirk Concannon must be made of solid wood from the neck up.

The next moment she was free and standing beside Jason. He had Morgan's wrist circled with one of his hands and the front of Dirk's shirt twisted securely in his other. "Morgan's through dancing for the night," he informed her startled partner tersely. "As a matter of fact, Concannon, she's through with you, period. And, the next time I see you, *if* I ever see you again, you had better be as far away from Morgan as possible."

"Jason!" she exclaimed, trying to contain her happiness over his obvious jealousy as he dragged her off the dance floor and over to a secluded corner of the room. "That was very rude."

"I'll tell you what's rude," Jason rounded fiercely on her once they had reached the relative isolation of the corner. "It's rude to allow one man to practically make love to you, when you're on a date with another man."

Observing that his eyes were almost black, Morgan told herself that she should be congratulated on her brilliant job of arousing him. But what had caused it? Passion? Anger? Or maybe it was simply a combination of both. Perhaps it didn't really matter. The important thing was she had gotten him to drop his attitude of cold indifference and to show some honest emotion.

The level of excitement between them had been steadily escalating all evening and now a familiar languor entered her bloodstream, causing her voice to give away her state. "You'd like to make love to me, wouldn't you, Jason?"

"Love doesn't enter into what I'd like to do to you, Morgan." His hold on her wrist tightened painfully.

"Then, you call it what you want, and I'll call it what I want. Words won't change anything."

"What I *want* is for you to give up, go away and leave me the hell alone."

"I can't believe that's what you really mean. I love you, Jason, and—"

"Don't say that!"

"All right," Morgan agreed softly, edging forward until her body rested against his and putting her free arm around his neck, "I won't tell you I love you. Instead I'll tell you how much I desire you and crave you." She pointed the end of her tongue and flicked it into the deep cleft of his chin. "Wanting someone so badly and not being able to have them is a living hell."

"What do you know about hell?" he jeered.

"Hell is really a very simple term to define, Jason. Hell is not having you." He tried to put some distance between them by taking a step backward, but Morgan followed. "I miss everything we had together in Martinique. We need to be that way again, to laugh, to play, to make love . . ."

"Stop it, Morgan! You don't know what you're saying."

Her eyes glistened with her love for him, and her voice cracked with longing. "Oh, Jason."

He looked down at her for a long, endless moment. "Damn you, Morgan Saunders. Damn you, damn you, damn you."

"I *am* damned without you."

"Come on," he choked. He propelled her forcefully out of the room, procuring their coats and putting hers on her, then pushing her outside into the cold, starless midnight toward his car.

He seated her, then stalked around to his side and got in, starting the car and allowing it to idle in order to warm it up.

For a long period of time that seemed to stretch to forever, Jason stared straight ahead into the darkness, apparently wrestling with the blackness of his thoughts and leaving Morgan to deal silently with her own. Even so, there was a highly charged awareness that streamed between them, making it impossible for one not to be aware of the other.

Suddenly and without warning, Jason turned. Grabbing the front of her coat with one hand, he jerked her to him and his lips came down on hers in a forcefully sensual kiss.

Morgan didn't even think about resisting. It

had been so long since Jason had kissed her and held her. All she could think about was that she had finally broken through his control. She had won . . . hadn't she?

His hand went inside her coat, delving into the neckline of her dress, feeling, exploring and kneading her breast as if he, too, had been starved for the touch of her. Leaving her breast, his hand skimmed restlessly down to her hips, descending and then ascending until it was high up under her skirt.

"My God," he ground out hoarsely. "You really *don't* have anything on under this dress."

"I don't lie, Jason."

For some reason, her shakily spoken words infuriated him. His fingers began to stroke her with a breathstopping imperativeness—not caring that they were in a parked car on a well-lit parking lot where anyone might happen to walk by—and all the while holding her fast to him.

Morgan pushed aside Jason's coat and fumblingly unbuttoned his shirt. Then, moving the top of her dress down to below her breasts, she leaned against his chest, glorying in the textural sensations of the coarse hairs that rasped against her.

Jason groaned, a sound that seemed to come straight from his soul. "You said that no one would know you didn't have any underwear on underneath this dress . . . maybe they didn't, but *I* did, and it worked on my mind—just as you knew it would. Everytime a man came near you tonight, I lost a little more of my sanity." His breath warmed her as he talked and dropped tiny, ravenous kisses all over her face. "And now I'm afraid you're going to have to pay the consequences."

Shoving her away with the exact same swiftness that he had brought her to him, Jason put the car in gear, and racing through the city streets, they reached his apartment in record time. Not a word had been spoken between them since they had left the parking lot, and Morgan wasn't sure what to expect. Jason wasn't acting quite as she had imagined he would. Where was the love and the gentleness he had showed to her in Martinique?

But once they were both in his apartment, some of the urgency that Morgan had sensed earlier seemed to leave him. He closed the door behind them and locked and bolted it with systematic care. Then leaning back against it, he made a thorough and devastating inspection of her.

She stood uncertainly, still wearing her coat, but Jason didn't change his position. He just stayed where he was for an endless length of time, observing her through slitted eyes. At last, just when Morgan's nerves were about ready to shatter, he pushed away from the door and moved toward her. Grasping the lapels of her coat, he took it off her, permitting it to fall to the floor.

Jason smiled, and a frigid shiver of alarm rushed down Morgan's spine. It was a smile unlike any he had ever given her and the dangerous intent of it was evident. She knew that he was a man who had been driven almost beyond his endurance, and his control had at last broken.

Laying the back of his hand against her chest,

he ran a finger inside her dress, rubbing it back and forth across her breast, exerting a light pressure, the tip of his finger barely brushing the erogenous rim of her nipple.

She loved Jason, she wanted him, she was on fire for him. Morgan slumped against him, but Jason pushed her upright, watching with an almost unreal detachment the longing expressions flit across her face.

All at once, he took a firm hold of the upper part of her dress and yanked. The beautiful garment tore in two pieces from top to bottom, and Morgan stood before him naked. Jason became motionless. His eyes touched every square inch of her, from the aquamarine iridescence of her eyes, to the lushness of her full mouth, down to the proud uplift of her breasts, on to the silky length of her legs, and on down to her toes.

When his gaze came back to her face, he stepped toward her, bringing his body into full contact with hers. Gripping her shoulders, his mouth brushed up and down her neck, tracing across her collarbone to the other side, where his mouth repeated his kissing actions.

Morgan could feel his pelvic hardness against her lower body and it excited her beyond belief. "Jason?"

His lips stayed at the base of her throat, feeling the rapid fire beat of her pulse. Taking a deep shuddering breath, his words sounded forced from the very depths of his being. "Lord help me, but I've got to have you."

He swept her into his arms and carried her into his bedroom, depositing her on the bed. Shedding his clothes with little attention to where they fell, he let his full weight come down on top of her, his mouth covering hers almost in the same instant. Morgan opened her mouth eagerly to the hot raspiness of his tongue and curled her legs around his back with a naturalness born of love and desire.

But there was no gentleness to Jason's touch. Instead, there was an urgent need, a naked hunger, a raw passion, and yes, a rage that was hurting them both.

His mouth roved impatiently over her face and then lower, to her breasts, fastening firmly onto the receptive tip. His teeth circled her breast in tiny nips, galvanizing electric bits of delight into her system. He sucked first one nipple, then the other, creating an intense and gratifying suction and bringing a helpless moan from Morgan.

The sound seemed to excite Jason further, and his lips nibbled down her stomach, halting between her legs where his tongue took over. He was consuming her, and it was plain that his need to taste all of her was acute.

Morgan's body was clamoring for his with a sizzling severity that exceeded anything she had felt for him before. Jason came back up to her mouth, crushing it with his, reaching his tongue deep into the sweet recess, until apparently he could wait no longer. Lifting his lower body, he probed the opening he sought, rubbing against her, until Morgan cried out her need.

Jason drove into her with an almost pagan savagery, time after time, and Morgan urged him on, more than meeting his demands with those of

her own. A hot, spiraling tension built quickly
until, in one tumultuous, paroxysmal burst, the
world the two of them had created came to an
end, and they were suspended together on a pla-
teau of almost unendurable pleasure.

Descending slowly, they fell asleep with their
bodies still joined.

Morgan awoke in the early hours before dawn
with the feeling that she was alone. Jason's body
was no longer lying curled around her, and it was
a loss she felt greatly. Her body felt incomplete
without his. Telling herself that he couldn't have
left her and that he had probably awakened hungry and was in the kitchen getting something to
eat, she stretched with a satisfied abandon and
rolled over.

Jason lay on the other side of the bed, awake
and staring at the ceiling. He must have felt her
movements, yet he didn't turn.

Watching him for a moment, a sense of unease
stole over her. Something was wrong, and Morgan asked quietly, "What is it that you see on the
ceiling?"

"You," he responded. "Everywhere there's you."

He still didn't look at her. His face was a chiseled profile, hard and dark. Morgan pursued. "Why
did you blush last night when I mouthed the
words, 'You're beautiful'? I had never seen you do
that before."

"Because . . . right at that moment, I had been
thinking the very same thing"—Jason's voice was
a monotone, colorless and dull—"and I was having to fight to keep myself from going to you."

"But you did anyway."

"Yes . . . I did." He turned his head toward her, and his words had a certain resigned flatness to them. "I couldn't stand to see that jerk's hands on you one more second."

Morgan mouth curved gently. "That proves that we belong together."

"Together in hell." It was a statement of fact.

"How about heaven?" Her smile broadened, trying to infuse lightheartedness into the heavy atmosphere. "I hear the climate is much better."

Jason reached across the bed and touched her mouth with his forefinger. "Why are you smiling?"

The strangeness of Jason's mood pervaded the bedroom, causing Morgan to stay where she was, and she answered him in a tone as solemn as his. "Because everything is going to be all right."

"You think so?"

"Yes. Things are working out between you and me, and when David gets back, we can all three sit down and talk. He'll be all right. You'll see."

"Shut up, Morgan." He reached for her and pulled her to him. "I'm not through with you yet." And this time, he made love to her with exquisite slowness, reminding her of their lovemaking in the rain forest. But when next she woke, she was alone again.

A momentary wall of despair hit her. Not again! she thought. She didn't think she could cope with even one more setback. Morgan felt as if she had been beating her head against a brick wall for far too long, and she was tired of the pain it was causing.

Muffled sounds from the other room soon reassured her that at least Jason was close by. Getting up from the bed, Morgan decided upon a shower. This time she was able to linger for as long as she wanted, the warm steam permeating the pores of her skin, opening them to the fragrant smell of Jason's soap.

Once again, she chose a black velour towel over the ever-present bathrobe, and, feeling refreshed, sauntered forth to find Jason.

Standing by the telephone, as if he had just completed a call, or was thinking of making a call, he was drinking a cup of coffee. The way his eyes followed her movements made Morgan slightly uncomfortable, but she stubbornly shrugged off the feeling.

"Good morning, darling." She pressed a kiss onto his cold cheek.

Jason took another sip of coffee and put the cup down. "You're looking beautiful, as always, Morgan. How *do* you manage it?"

His words were a compliment, but the intonation was something else. Morgan shook her head. "Lucky genes, I suppose." Noticing that a mist of heat still rose from his cup, she raised it to her lips. "Do you mind?" she inquired, taking a drink of the bracing black liquid.

"Not at all, Morgan. By all means, help yourself to anything of mine that happens to take your fancy."

She had been walking toward the couch, but now she turned around. "I beg your pardon?" Again, it wasn't so much the words, as it had been the tone.

"You heard me."

Morgan sat down, eyeing Jason's granitelike

countenance with a profound sadness. Here it was, then. Even after everything she had done, it wasn't going to work. Nothing had really changed between them, except that they had made love. She exhaled wearily. "I gather there's something in particular you're referring to?"

"Not *something,* sweetheart. You've seduced me so effectively, that as far as I'm concerned, you can have any or all of my possessions. They don't matter. I'll give you the key to my bank vault tomorrow if you wish."

"Then what are we talking about, Jason? I'm not a mindreader. Apparently, there's something still between us that we need to talk about."

"Correction. *Someone.* David, to be more precise."

"David?"

"That's right," he taunted. "Tell me, Morgan, does it make you feel good to be sleeping with two brothers. Is it some kind of kinky turn-on for you?"

She paled. "I-I don't know what you're talking about, Jason."

"Don't play the innocent with me," Jason growled. "You forget. I've been to bed with you, Morgan. I know there's nothing of the innocent in you."

"I still don't understand." A hint of anger rose in Morgan's voice. "If you're talking about the uninhibited way I make love with you . . . that's only with you. There's no one else. I love you, Jason, only you."

Jason walked over to her, grasping her by the shoulders and lifting her to him. Low and husky came his reply. "Oh, you don't have to worry. The fact that you've been my brother's lover doesn't matter anymore. It can't. I want you too badly, and, to my own great peril, I have found that I can't possibly live without you."

"J-Jason—"

"You can relax. You've won. But," he warned harshly, "there'll be no more David. That has to be understood . . . by both of you. It won't be an ideal family unit, of course, but then very little in life is ever as perect as we would wish."

Morgan broke away from Jason's hold, moving a little ways away and rubbing her skin where his bruising hold had gripped her. "Let me get this perfectly straight." An awful calm had settled within her. No more panic. No more desperation. After all these weeks, she finally understood.

"You think that David and I have been lovers, that I lied to you when I told you—both in spoken words and the ones written in my letter—that there was nothing serious between David and me. And further you think that once I found out David was your brother, I slept with you just for the kick of sleeping with two brothers." Morgan paused and drew a deep breath. "Does that about sum it up, Jason?"

His stony expression had changed imperceptibly, but he still nodded his agreement.

"I see." Morgan escaped the room as quickly as she could. Sitting on Jason's bed, she wrapped her arms around her waist, trying to instill strength into her wobbling limbs.

Her mind cast backward over the past few months, trying to reason out why Jason had received the impression he had. She kept coming back to the same thing, though. He couldn't have jumped to that conclusion—not on his own. It was impossible. He must have had what he considered undisputable proof. But what?

David. David must have said something . . . in some unknowing way suggested . . . But how? Again, her mind replayed the events of the last few months, the months before she had flown to Martinique and met Jason.

Her thoughts halted. *New York*. David had gone to New York with her and they had stayed in the same hotel. David must have mentioned the trip to Jason and he had taken it for granted that she and David had slept together. It was the only answer that made any sense.

How could Jason even think such a thing of her? her heart cried, but her brain reasoned, *thinking that*, it was no wonder he had treated her with such scorn these last few weeks.

Morgan picked up the phone and punched out Jerome's number. He answered and she was exceedingly glad to hear a friendly, uncomplicated voice.

"Jerome? How long will it take you to come pick me up?"

He must have heard the quavering note in her voice, because he didn't ask any unnecessary questions. "Where are you?"

"Jason's."

"I can be there in fifteen minutes."

"Great. Make it ten and I'll be down in front of his building waiting for you."

"Morgan . . . are you all right?"

"No, Jerome, I'm not."

Shedding the towel, Morgan found her coat in an untidy heap on a chair and put it on. It was the only thing she had in the way of clothes.

Moving slowly back out into the living room, Morgan ran shaking fingers through her hair, fanning the ash-blond strands over her shoulders. Jason was still there, standing where she had left him.

Mentally squaring her shoulders, Morgan said, "I'm going to tell you the facts one more time, Jason. So listen well, because after this, it will be up to you. The truth of the matter is that David and I were never lovers. It is true that David believed he was serious about me, but I *never*, in any way, encouraged him—and I think that when David gets back from wherever it is that you've sent him, he'll confirm it.

"I've tried to figure out how in the world you got the idea that David and I were lovers, and since you assure me that your brother doesn't lie, I can come up with only one thing. The last time I had to go to New York on a buying trip, David insisted, since he had to go there on business, too, that we might as well go together. He felt that if we stayed at the same hotel, we would be able to dine together each evening. *However*, we stayed ten floors apart, and at no time did we sleep together.

"My only sin, as I see it, was being too soft with David, and of that I plead guilty. By trying so hard not to hurt his feelings, by thinking that given enough time, David's crush on me would pass, I ended up causing myself more grief than I ever thought possible. Then, again," she added cynically, "I never expected to fall in love with a man as untrusting as you."

Morgan started toward the door, but then stopped and turned back. Jason's eyes were on her and there was a curious look of grief on his face.

Unlike the evening before, Morgan could summon no sympathy for him. "And there's one more thing you need to know. I'd get down on my knees if it would help, Jason. I love you that much. But I can't *force* you to believe me, and I'm sick and tired of playing games. I won't be bothering you again." She gave a sad little laugh. "It seems you weren't the man I thought you were after all."

Ten

Jerome was waiting for her, the car idling at the curb. "Drive," Morgan commanded, "and don't stop until I say."

Jerome took one look at her tear-stained face and did as she said. Speaking only of the unimportant matters that truly good friends manage to talk about in times of trouble, yet, at the same time, convey their complete support for the other, Morgan and Jerome covered all the trivia bases, from baseball and football to the weather and the shop. A couple of hours later, Morgan realized they must have driven the route around the city more than once.

"I think I'm ready to go home now. Besides, I imagine we're just about out of gas, aren't we?"

"We ran out of gas a few miles back." Jerome grinned, unperturbed.

"Wonderful. Should I start worrying?"

"Nope. I've got this car on a rigid schedule. It's trained to go from paycheck to paycheck without a fillup. It can even run on fumes if necessary."

"That's great, but your car's schedule probably doesn't include a marathon drive around the city. I've been so involved with Jason that I've forgotten when your next paycheck is, but I hope it's soon because I don't think we're going to make it."

In the end, Sami had to come pick them up in her vintage MG roadster. Because the car's top didn't work, Sami could only take it out when it wasn't snowing or raining. Ordinary frigid Minnesota winter weather had never been known to stop her, though.

Tucking a heavy blanket around Morgan, just as if she were a patient in shock and had to be kept warm, Sami scolded, "I've been out of my mind with worry, Morgan. First you didn't come home last night, which was really okay because I knew who you were with, and then Jerome goes to pick you up and the two of you disappear for hours. And anyway, why didn't you call *me* to pick you up?"

"Because you never answer your phone."

"That's no excuse! You knew I'd be waiting to hear all about your date."

"I think we need to look into a system of carrier pigeons," Morgan proposed dryly.

"Pigeons I could relate to—telephones, on the other hand, are such cold, impersonal instruments."

Morgan laughed at Sami. "As for my date, like

the ABC sports' announcer says, it was 'the thrill of victory, and the agony of defeat.' "

"What? There's something wrong with your feet?" Sami didn't watch television.

"Not my feet . . . my heart. I've told Jason that he won't be seeing me again, and I meant it. The only problem is that I still love the rat."

"That may not be such a problem," Sami beamed. "Jason's been pacing the floor of your apartment for a couple of hours now."

Morgan looked at Sami. "Are you serious?"

"Never more so. And believe it or not, he looks worse than you do. That must have been some night the two of you had."

"More like the morning," Morgan mumbled, rummaging in her purse for a mirror.

She opened the door of her apartment with mixed feelings. Tired of trying to second-guess Jason, she was at the point where she wanted things between them settled one way or the other.

He stood by the window. Sami had been right. He looked even paler than she felt.

"Morgan! Where have you been? I've been half out of my mind with worry."

As she closed the door her answer came out with an amount of pain that surprised even her. "What's the matter, Jason? Were you afraid I had decided to take my life over you? You needn't have worried. I might have thought about killing *you* on occasion, but never myself. Messy business, suicide, anyway, and it hurts no one but the person who does it."

"Morgan." He crossed the room to take her hands in his. "We need to talk."

"That plea sounds vaguely familiar. I wonder where I could have heard it?" She withdrew her hands from his. "At any rate, I'm not doing a thing until I get out of this coat and into some clothes. I seem to have lost my dress."

Once again, Jason surprised her by blushing. "I'm sorry about that."

She looked at him dispassionately. "I don't seem to be the only one with a bag full of tricks. That blush of yours is very disarming."

"I don't do it on purpose, Morgan!"

"It doesn't matter," she murmured, her sense of humor returning somewhat at his defiant tone. Men! When you came right down to it, were they anything more than big babies? "Make yourself at home. I'll be back in a minute."

In her room, she donned a pair of navy trousers and a pastel blue-green silk blouse. Taking the time to comb out the tangles that the winter wind had whipped into her hair, she also applied a softly tinted gloss to her lips.

Returning to her living room, she found Jason still standing, looking satisfyingly uncomfortable. Choosing her most comfortable chair, she sank onto its thick pillowed upholstery. "Okay, Jason. You've got the floor."

There was a surprising uncertainty to his stance and a vaguely hesitant quality to his words. "I'm not sure if you'll ever be able to forgive me, Morgan, but I know now that I've been wrong, terribly wrong."

Returning his gaze levely, Morgan remarked

coolly, "That's very interesting, Jason. It's taken you long enough to come to that conclusion. What has changed?"

A heartfelt gladness had commenced to stir in her, but there was no way she was going to make this easy for him. She had to make sure of *what* he was saying and *why*.

"Nothing, I suppose. You see, I fell in love with you so quickly and so easily, that maybe subconsciously I didn't really trust what had happened to us. It all seemed so simple. Yet I had never known such happiness. I felt as if I could have flown back to St. Paul without a plane.

"But when I got home and David started telling me all about this wonderful girl he was in love with and was going to marry, I couldn't believe it. I didn't completely until you walked in his office door and he took you in his arms. And unfortunately, he had already mentioned the New York trip. Probably the only reason I hadn't heard about you before was because he and I had been going in different directions for the last few months, and when we did get together, we only had time for business.

"When he finally did tell me, I'm afraid blind jealousy took over my common sense, coupled with a sincere worry about David. I told you, I've felt a responsibility toward him for a long time now, and we're very close."

"Poor baby. You were so crushed that you immediately made a date with Melinda whats-her-name."

"Melinda Johnson is a very nice lady and an old friend of the family."

"She didn't look that old to me," Morgan observed spitefully.

"Ah-ha!" Jason pounced. "So you were jealous, too."

Squirming in her chair, Morgan hedged, "Not really. She just didn't seem to be your type, that's all."

His eyebrows quirked. "My type being?"

"Me, of course."

Jason's voice softened. "Morgan, she's in love with David and has been for a long time. I was simply trying to comfort her, because she had found out that David had gone away and *why*."

"And did you? Comfort her, that is?"

"I told her where to find David. I'm sure by now that Melinda has been able to console David and he's realized that it's been her all along that he really loves. I expect we'll be receiving some happy news from them soon."

"I'm just a sucker for happy endings."

Ignoring her sarcastically mumbled sentence, Jason lifted her from the chair and into his arms. "Well, then, have *I* got a happy ending for you."

His kisses covered her face and lips, and when at last he drew away, both of them were left breathless.

Morgan pulled back. "You haven't told me why you've decided you believed me. You *do* believe me now, don't you?"

Not letting her escape his hold altogether, he answered, "I believe you. Deep down, I think I've always known there had to be a logical reason why your story and David's story didn't match. But there were so many emotions and conflicts fighting inside me: My love for David, my jealousy of David, my fury that you might have lied to me, my grief that I couldn't have you—but most of all, my love for you.

"You kept telling me to remember. The problem was I couldn't forget. And in saner moments, I was already beginning to doubt my judgment. There's a startling purity and innocence that shone out of you, even when you were doing all the perfectly outrageous things that you were doing.

"I knew the minute you walked out the door this morning that you weren't lying. The only reason I didn't fully realize it before was that I was a blind fool."

She gave him a half-smile. "I'm not about to argue with that."

"I love you, Morgan. There were times when I thought I wouldn't survive being apart from you, and of course, your aggressively feminine seduction of me didn't help matters any."

"You deserved it," she told him righteously.

"Maybe," he replied, amused. "At any rate, there'll be no more resistance on my part. Seduce away."

"Gosh"—Morgan was picking at a button on his shirt—"that'll sort of take the fun out of it."

"Want to bet?" he teased, then returned to a serious tone. "Please forgive me, Morgan. If you will, I promise I'll spend the rest of my life making it up to you."

"Wellll . . ."

"I know a perfect place for a honeymoon," he prompted.

"I'll have to think about it. I've sort of become

partial to one particular Caribbean island." Morgan's blue-green eyes glittered with love.

"Funny. That's just what I was thinking. Does that mean you'll marry me?"

"Why of course, Jason," Morgan replied meekly, "if you insist."

Martinique enjoyed a beautiful spring that year, and Morgan and Jason spent their honeymoon in a cottage on the Frontenac Plantation. And if Roger and Serge thought it was strange that their two favorite guests didn't emerge from their cottage for long periods at a time, they didn't say a word.

THE EDITOR'S CORNER

While you anticipate a warm, wonderful Thanksgiving with your family and friends, you can also look forward to a warm, wonderful (but not fattening!) time with the LOVESWEPT books for November.

First there's **BREAKFAST IN BED**, LOVESWEPT #22, by Sandra Brown. A reader wrote to us about Sandra's LOVESWEPT launch book, #1, HEAVEN'S PRICE: "Simply wonderful! Just the right blend of sensuality and romance, kissed with humor." Well, all those ingredients in Sandra's work come together yet again— or should I say as always?—in her sizzling love story BREAKFAST IN BED. From the moment that famous mystery novelist Carter Madison steps foot into Sloan Fairchild's bed and breakfast inn, both of them are goners! Their attraction for one another is fierce, open . . . and impossible. As the days pass, their rising need for one another physically is only surpassed by their growing love for one another as unique individuals. Tethered by exquisite bonds of other love and loyalty, they cannot reach out—until fate intervenes so that fulfillment may follow. BREAKFAST IN BED is vibrantly sensual, and truly touching emotionally.

For new author Becky Combs the best part of **TAKING SAVANNAH**, #23, may be her own true love story that came about because of this novel.

(continued)

While researching the background of TAKING SAVAN-NAH, Becky took a carriage ride through the historic section of Savannah—and that carriage ride changed her life. She was using her tape recorder and the carriage driver asked about it. When Becky explained that she was looking into the restoration and preservation of the town's historic houses, the driver told her about an architect she should interview. Ah-hh, believe it or not Becky and that architect met, fell in love, and will be married this November—to celebrate the publication of this book and the reason for their meeting. TAKING SAVANNAH is an absolute delight! And, I ask you, can you resist a romance novel that led to romance in real life?

Ooo-la-la! Here's another Iris Johansen love story! And I know that's going to please you because we've received an overwhelming amount of mail praising Iris's first two LOVESWEPT romances. What a fan club is forming for this new author who is so talented at telling magical tales of love! Now, in **THE RELUCTANT LARK**, #24, you'll find yet another incredibly emotional story which you won't be able to put down. Rand Challon is a hero with whom every one of us on the LOVESWEPT staff has fallen madly in love—while being entranced with heroine Sheena Reardon. In this powerfully gripping romance, we see Sheena, an American-Irish folk singer, grow into womanhood under Rand's passionate tutelage. We learn the meaning behind her haunting ballad, "Rory's Song." We root for her as she makes an unnerving series of choices . . . and, as our copyeditor expressed it, "at the end you just feel like standing up and cheering!"

All the LOVESWEPT authors and staff join me in wishing you a *very* happy Thanksgiving.

With all warm wishes,

Carolyn Nichols

Carolyn Nichols
   Editor
LOVESWEPT
Bantam Books, Inc.
666 Fifth Avenue
New York, NY 10103

Love Stories you'll never forget by authors you'll always remember

THE LATEST BOOKS
IN THE BANTAM
BESTSELLING TRADITION